"I don't know why I just told you all that..." Mackenzie said to fill the silence.

While Mackenzie was telling her story, it reminded Dylan of the girl she had once been. The girl he remembered so vividly from his childhood—the chubby bookworm with thick glasses. All the boys in the neighborhood ignored her, but he never had. He had never thought to analyze why. He had always just liked Mackenzie.

"Because we used to be friends," Dylan said.

"Were we?" Mackenzie asked.

"I always thought so." Dylan caught her gaze and held it. "And I tell you this, Mackenzie. If I had known that you were pregnant...if you had just trusted me enough to give me a chance, I never would've let you or Hope go through any of this stuff alone. I would have been there for you...both of you...every step of the way."

Dear Reader,

Thank you for choosing *Marry Me, Mackenzie!* Mackenzie and Dylan's love story is the third in the Brand Family line (following *A Baby for Christmas* and *The One He's Been Looking For*). Writing Mackenzie and Dylan's romance was a real pleasure for me.

Dylan Axel played a significant role in *The One He's Been Looking For* as Ian Sterling's best friend, and I knew, from the very beginning, that he was definitely a Harlequin hero. He's a loyal friend, an entrepreneur, handsome, athletic and one hundred percent husband material. So, it was really just a matter of time before Dylan scored his own story. I had already planned a story for Mackenzie Brand, and when it was time to start writing, I realized that Dylan was her perfect match!

And, I just couldn't resist setting another story in my favorite city, San Diego. San Diego is a sophisticated city with a supercool bohemian-artsy atmosphere that I totally dig! After I honeymooned there with my husband, I knew that it was a perfect place for my characters to fall in love.

I sincerely hope that you enjoy reading *Marry Me, Mackenzie!*, and if you want to catch up with the rest of the Brand clan, *A Baby for Christmas* and *The One He's Been Looking For* are still available. Be sure to stay tuned for more Brand Family romance coming out in 2015...

Happy reading!

*Joanna Sims*

# Marry Me, Mackenzie!

——

## Joanna Sims

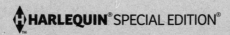
HARLEQUIN® SPECIAL EDITION®

Recycling programs
for this product may
not exist in your area.

ISBN-13: 978-0-373-65869-5

Marry Me, Mackenzie!

Copyright © 2015 by Joanna Sims

**Printed in U.S.A.**

**Joanna Sims** lives in Florida with her awesome husband, Cory, and their three fabulous felines, Sebastian, Chester (aka Tubby) and Ranger. By day, Joanna works as a speech-language pathologist, and by night, she writes contemporary romance for Harlequin Special Edition. Joanna loves to hear from Harlequin readers and invites you to stop by her website for a visit: joannasimsromance.com

### Books by Joanna Sims

### Harlequin Special Edition

*The One He's Been Looking For*
*A Baby for Christmas*

Visit the Author Profile page at Harlequin.com for more titles.

Dedicated to Aunt Gerri and Uncle Bill

You are loved more than words can say!

## *Chapter One*

Mackenzie Brand parallel parked her 1960 Chevy sedan and shut off the engine. She leaned against the steering wheel and looked through the windshield at the swanky condos that lined Mission Beach, California. She checked the address that her cousin, Jordan, had given her and matched it with the address on the white, trilevel condo on the left. With a sigh, she unbuckled her seat belt and slipped the key out of the ignition.

"All right. Not exactly your crowd. But a job's a job and a favor's a favor." Mackenzie got out of her car, locked the door and dropped the keys into her Go Green recycling tote bag. She could hear a mixture of classic rock, loud talking and laughing as she walked quickly to the front door. It sounded like the Valentine's Day party that Jordan was throwing with her fiancé, Ian, was already in full swing.

Mackenzie rang the doorbell twice and then knocked on the door. While she waited, she stared down at her holey black Converse sneakers. They had passed shabby chic several months ago—definitely time to get a new pair. After a few minutes spent contemplating her pitiful tennis shoes, Mackenzie pressed the doorbell again. When no one opened the door, Mackenzie turned around to head to the beach side of the condo. She was about to step down the first step when she heard the door open.

"Hey!" Dylan Axel swung the front door open wide. "Where're you going?"

Dylan's voice, a voice Mackenzie hadn't heard in a very long time, reverberated up her spine like an old forgotten song. Mackenzie simultaneously twisted her torso toward Dylan while taking a surprised step back. Her eyes locked with his for a split second before she lost her balance and began to fall backward.

"Hey…" Dylan saw the pretty brunette at his door begin to fall. He sprang forward and grabbed one of her flailing arms. "Careful!"

Silent and wide-eyed, Mackenzie clutched the front of Dylan's shirt to steady herself. Dylan pulled her body toward his and for a second or two, she was acutely aware of everything about the man: the soapy scent of his skin, the strong, controlled grasp of his fingers on her arm, the dark chest hair visible just above the top button of his designer shirt.

"Are you okay?" Dylan asked. He didn't know who she was, but she smelled like a sugar cookie and had beautiful Elizabeth Taylor eyes.

If he hadn't caught her, she would have fallen for sure. Could have seriously injured herself. And Mackenzie's body knew it. Her heart was pounding in her chest, her skin felt prickly and hot, and her equilibrium was off-kilter. Mackenzie closed her eyes for a moment, took in a steadying breath, before she slowly released the death grip she had on his shirt.

"I'm fine," Mackenzie said stiffly. "Thank you."

"Are you sure?"

Mackenzie nodded. She forced herself to focus her eyes straight ahead on the single silver hair on Dylan's chest instead of looking up into his face.

"You can let go now." Mackenzie tugged her arm away from Dylan's hand.

Dylan immediately released her arm, hands up slightly as if he were being held up at gunpoint. "Sorry about that."

Mackenzie self-consciously tugged on the front of her oversize Nothin' But Cupcakes T-shirt. "No, *I'm* sorry."

Dylan smiled at her. "Let's just call it even, okay?"

That was classic Dylan; always trying to smooth things over with a smile. He wasn't as lanky as he had been in his early twenties. His body had filled out, but he was fit and had the lean body of an avid California surfer. And he still had that boyish, easygoing smile and all-American good looks. Even back in middle school, Dylan had been popular with absolutely everyone. Male or female, it didn't matter. He had always been effortlessly charming and approachable. Right then, on Dylan's porch, the last ten years melted away for Mackenzie, but she knew that he obviously hadn't recognized her.

Still smiling, Dylan stuck out his hand to her. "I'm Dylan. And you are?"

Instead of taking his offered hand or responding, Mackenzie stared at him mindlessly. It felt as if all of her blood had drained out of her head and rushed straight to her toes.

*I'm not ready for this...*

Dylan's smile faded slightly. He gave her a curious look and withdrew his hand. "You must be one of Jordan's friends. Why don't you come in so we can track 'er down."

Mackenzie was screaming in her mind, demanding that her stubborn legs take a step forward as she plastered a forced smile on her face.

"Thank you." She squeaked out the platitude as she skirted by Dylan and into the condo.

"Mackenzie!" Jordan wound her way through the crowd of people gathered in the living room and threw her arms around her cousin. "Thank *God* you could come! You're the *best*, do you know that?"

"Jordan!" Relieved, Mackenzie hugged her cousin. "Okay—first things first—I have to see this ring in person."

Jordan held out her hand and wiggled her finger so her large cushion-cut blue diamond engagement ring caught the light.

"Jordan, it's beautiful." Mackenzie held Jordan's left hand loosely while she admired the large blue diamond.

"I know, right? It's ridiculous." Jordan beamed. "It's way too extravagant. Ian really shouldn't have…but I'm glad he did."

"Dylan." Jordan draped her arm across Mackenzie's shoulders. "*This* is my *awesome* cousin, Mackenzie. She owns Nothin' But Cupcakes, home of the famous giant cupcakes. Look it up." To Mackenzie she said, "Thank you again for bringing us emergency cupcakes."

"Of course." Mackenzie kept her eyes trained on her cousin in order to avoid making eye contact with Dylan. For the first time in a long time, she wished she still had her thick tortoiseshell glasses to hide behind.

"Mackenzie—this's Dylan Axel… Dylan is the *Axel* in Sterling and Axel Photography. He's also a certified investment planner. He totally has the Midas touch with money, so if you ever need financial advice for your business, he's your man."

Mackenzie had to make a concerted effort to breathe normally and braced herself for Dylan to recognize her. But when she did finally shift her eyes to his, Dylan still didn't show even a *flicker* of recognition. He didn't seem to have the *first clue* that he was being introduced to a woman he had known in the *biblical* sense of the word. Instead, he looked between them with a slightly perplexed expression on his good-looking face. No doubt, he was wondering how she had managed to sneak into gorgeous Jordan's gene pool.

"Now I know your name." Dylan held out his hand to her once more. "Mackenzie."

The way Dylan lingered on her name sent her heart palpitating again. He was looking at her in the way a man looks at a woman he finds attractive. Dylan had never looked at her this way before. It was…*unsettling*. And yet, *validating*. It was undeniable proof that she had truly managed to eradicate the obese preteen with Coke-bottle glasses and tangled, mousy hair that she had once been.

Mackenzie forced herself to maintain the appearance of calm when she slipped her hand into his. She quickly shook his hand and then tucked her hand away in her pocket. Inside her pocket, where no one could see, Mackenzie balled up her fingers into a tight fist.

Oblivious to her cousin's discomfort, Jordan rested her arm across Mackenzie's shoulders. "Do you need help bringing in the cupcakes?"

Mackenzie nodded. "You wanted a ton. You got a ton."

Jordan walked with Mackenzie through the still-open front door. She tossed over her shoulder, "Give us a hand, Dylan, will you?"

"We can manage," Mackenzie protested immediately.

"I'm not about to let you ladies do all the heavy lifting by yourselves," Dylan said as he trailed behind them.

As they approached her car, Dylan whistled appreciatively. It was no surprise; men always commented on her car.

"The 1960 Chevrolet Biscayne Delivery Sedan painted with the original factory turquoise from back in the day. *Nice.*" Dylan ran his hand lovingly over the hood of her car. "She's yours?"

Mackenzie nodded quickly before she walked to the back of the delivery sedan; she unlocked, and then lifted up, the heavy back hatch of the vehicle.

"Who did this restoration?" Dylan asked as he leaned down and looked at the interior of the Chevy.

"A place up near Sacramento." Mackenzie wanted to be vague. Her brother, Jett, who had restored her Chevy at his hot-rod shop, had been friends with Dylan back in middle school. In fact, the last time Mackenzie had seen Dylan Axel was *at* Jett's wedding nearly eleven years ago.

"Well—they did an insane job. This car is *beautiful.* I'd really like to take a look under her hood."

"Hey!" Jordan poked her head around the back of the car. "Are you gonna help us out here, Axel, or what?"

"I'm helping." Dylan laughed as he strolled to the back of the vehicle. "But you can't blame a guy for looking, now, can you?"

"Here. Make yourself useful, will ya?" Jordan rolled her eyes at him as she handed him a large box of cupcakes. "And, no, I don't get the obsession with cars that went out of production *decades* ago. They don't make them anymore for a *reason.* Now, if you want to get excited about a motorcycle, I can totally relate to that!"

Dylan took the box from Jordan but smiled at Mackenzie. "Well—your cousin gets it, don't you?"

Mackenzie looked directly into Dylan's oh-so-familiar crystal-clear green eyes for a split second. "I get it."

"See!" Dylan smiled triumphantly at Jordan. "She gets it."

"Well—sure. Her dad and brother raised Mackenzie in a garage. Basically, she's been brainwashed. No offense, cuz."

"None taken." Mackenzie balanced the large cupcake box in the crook of her arm while she pulled down the heavy hatch door. Mackenzie gave the hatch door a bump with her hip to shut it completely.

"Okay," Mackenzie said, wanting to speed things along. "Let's get the troops out of the sun."

Dylan kept pace with her as they walked back to the condo. "I haven't heard someone say that since I was a kid."

"Really?" Mackenzie pretended to be fascinated with the neighbor's house. "I hear it all the time."

That was one of her father's favorite phrases; no doubt, Dylan had heard him use it a zillion times before he moved away from the neighborhood. Her father had restored vintage cars as a hobby in the garage behind her childhood home, and all of the neighborhood boys, including Dylan, had loved to hang out with him.

"This works." Jordan put her box down on the large marble slab island that separated the kitchen from the great room.

Mackenzie put her box down next to Jordan's and started to formulate an exit strategy. Dylan opened the top of his box and reached for a cupcake. Jordan slapped his hand playfully and put the box lid back down.

"Get your sticky paws off the cupcakes, mister! Ian isn't even here yet! I can't believe he's late for his own party."

"I'm still surprised he agreed to this at all," Dylan said. "You know Ian hates crowds."

"No. You're right. He does. But I'm determined to pull

that man out of his shell kicking and screaming if I have to." Jordan pulled her phone out of the back pocket of her dark-wash skinny jeans. To Mackenzie she said, "Give me a sec, okay? I want to see what's holding him up. The two of you haven't even met each other yet."

Jordan plugged one ear and held the phone to the other as she headed outside to call her fiancé. Even though there was a large group of people milling around in the great room, using it as a pass-through to the bathrooms or the deck outside, at the moment, Mackenzie and Dylan were the only two people in the kitchen. Dylan sent her a conspiratorial wink as he lifted the box top and snagged one of her giant cupcakes.

Dylan devoured the devil's food cupcake in three bites. "These are incredible. Did you make these?"

Mackenzie nodded. "There's another cupcake designer who works for me, but these are mine."

Dylan grabbed a second cupcake and sent Mackenzie a questioning look. "I can count on you not to tell Jordan, right?"

"She *is* my cousin," Mackenzie said as she scratched her arm under her long-sleeved shirt. Being around Dylan again was making her skin feel itchy and hot.

"Good call," Dylan said before he bit into the second cupcake. "You gotta pick family over some random guy you just met. I understand."

Before she could respond, a statuesque Cameron Diaz look-alike in a tiny bikini breezed into the kitchen like she owned it.

"Babe," Jenna said as she dropped a quick kiss on Dylan's cheek, "we're running out of ice out there *already*."

"Okay. I'll run down to the store and grab some more," Dylan said before he took another bite.

Jenna opened the refrigerator and pulled out a can of

diet cola. She popped the top, took a sip and put the can on the counter.

"Hi," she said to Mackenzie and then moved on.

Dylan gave his girlfriend a "look" and handed her a coaster to put under the can. Jenna rolled her eyes, but put the coaster beneath the can. Then she crossed her arms over her chest, her pretty face registering a combination of disbelief and disgust.

"Babe—*what* are you *eating*?" Jenna frowned at him.

"Cupcakes." Dylan took another bite of the giant cupcake and pushed a box toward his girlfriend. "Want one?"

"Are you *insane*?" Jenna asked, horrified. "Carbs, Dylan! I've got an audition tomorrow in LA—the last thing I want to be is all *puffy* and *bloated*. I don't know how you can put that poison into your body anyway."

"Happily." Dylan winked at Mackenzie.

"Whatever." Jenna walked to the door. She paused in the doorway and yelled, "Ice!"

"Got it." Dylan didn't look at Jenna as he wolfed down the final bite of the cupcake.

Instead of leaving to get ice, Dylan stayed with her in the kitchen. "So—did you grow up in Montana, too?"

Mackenzie looked up at Dylan—one part of her wanted to exit stage left without saying a word, but the other part wanted to rip off the Band-Aid and get the inevitable out of the way. It wasn't a matter of *if* she would confront Dylan about their past—it was a matter of *when*. She was impatient by nature, so perhaps, *when* she should bring up their past was *right now*.

Gripping the side of the kitchen counter to hold her body steady, Mackenzie asked quietly, "You don't recognize me, do you?"

Dylan's brow dropped and a question mark came into

his eyes. He stared at her face hard, and she could almost see the wheels in his brain turning, trying to place her.

"You're not going to believe this, you guys." Jordan threw her hands up into the air as she walked into the kitchen. "He's stuck at the studio—his editor needs him to do something for the new book. He won't be here for *at least* another hour." Jordan's shoulders sagged as she asked Mackenzie, "You can hang out that long, can't you? I've been so busy with my gallery show that I've hardly spent any time with you—"

"I really can't stay." Mackenzie shook her head. "I have to get back to the bakery."

"What a drag." Jordan sighed. "I know, I know…business first. Ian's *exactly* the same way."

"I'll text you," Mackenzie promised. "We'll figure out when we can sync our calendars."

"Okay. It's a plan," Jordan agreed as she hugged her cousin one last time. "Give Hope a kiss for me."

"I will." Mackenzie glanced nervously at Dylan, who hadn't stopped staring at her. Jordan's phone rang. She checked the number. "It's the caterer. Let me grab this first and then I'll walk you out."

"Don't worry about it." Dylan, still staring hard at Mackenzie's face, said to Jordan, "I'll walk her out."

"You're all right, Dylan—I don't care what they say about you." Jordan punched Dylan lightly on the arm, and then gave Mackenzie one last parting hug before she answered the call.

Mackenzie could feel Dylan's intent gaze on her as they walked the short distance to the front door. Dylan opened the door for her.

"You say we've met?" Dylan asked curiously after he shut the front door behind him.

Dylan studied the petite, curvy woman walking beside

him and he tried to figure out who she was before she had to tell him. He had had a lot of drunken hookups when he was in college and he hoped that she wasn't one of them.

It seemed to Mackenzie that her heart was pumping way too much blood, too quickly, through her veins. She was light-headed and for a split second, as she was coming down the front steps, it felt as if she might just pass out.

*This is happening. After all these years. This is really happening.*

"Yes. We've met," Mackenzie said as she walked quickly to her car, unlocked the door and then opened it so she would have something to lean on.

"You were good friends with my brother, Jett, back in middle school." Mackenzie gripped the frame of the open car door so hard that her fingers started to hurt.

"Jett...?" Dylan shook his head slightly as if he didn't connect with the name, but then recognition slowly started to dawn as a smile started to move across his face.

"Wait a minute!" Dylan exclaimed. "*Big Mac*? Is that you?"

Mackenzie blanched. No one had called her that horrible nickname since high school.

"I don't like to be called that," she said. When she was growing up, no one called her "Mackenzie." Jett and her friends always called her "Mac." Cruel kids at school had added the "Big" to it and the horrible nickname had followed her like a black cloud until she graduated from high school.

"Hey—I'm sorry. I didn't mean anything by it." He couldn't stop staring at her face. This was not the Mackenzie he remembered. The thick, old-lady glasses were gone, her hair was darker and longer, and she had slimmed down. She wasn't skinny; she was curvy, which was a pretty rare occurrence in California. The word *voluptuous* popped into his head to describe her now.

"Just don't call me that anymore, okay?"

"Yeah. Sure. Never again, I promise," Dylan promised, his eyes smiling at her. "Man. I can't believe it…Jett's little sister! You look great."

"Thanks," Mackenzie said.

"Man…" Dylan crossed his arms loosely in front of his body and shook his head. "How long has it been? Five, six years?"

"Ten," Mackenzie said too quickly and then added more nonchalantly, "Give or take."

"Ten years." Dylan nodded as he tried to remember the last time he had seen her. When it hit him, he snapped his fingers. "Jett's wedding, right? I can't believe I didn't recognize you right away—but, in my defense, Mackenzie, you've changed."

"Yeah, well…losing a hundred pounds will do that to a person," Mackenzie said. She was watching him closely; it still didn't seem to be registering with him that they had slept together after Jett's reception.

"A hundred pounds?" he repeated, surprised. "I don't remember you needing to lose that much."

"You'd be one of the few." Mackenzie heard that old defensiveness creep into her tone.

Several seconds of silence slipped by before Dylan asked, "So—how's Jett doing nowadays? Still married?"

"Uh-uh." Mackenzie shook her head. "The marriage didn't work out. But he's got custody of both kids, so that's the upside of that situation."

"Does he live around here, too?"

"No. He owns a hot-rod shop up in Paradise, California. He wanted to be closer to Dad and he thought a small town would be better for the girls."

"A hot-rod shop, huh? So wait a minute—did Jett do this restoration?" Dylan asked with a nod toward her car.

"Yep." Mackenzie nodded proudly. Her older brother had managed to build a lucrative career out of a passion he shared with their dad.

"Man—I'm telling you what, he did a *fantastic* job on this Chevy. I really respect that he kept it true to the original design. I've gotta tell you, this's pretty amazing timing running into you like this because I've been looking for someone to restore my Charger. I gotta get her out of storage and back out on the road."

"You should check out his website—High-Octane Hot Rods."

"High-Octane Hot Rods. I'll do that." Dylan hadn't stopped smiling at her since he'd realized she was Jett's little sister. "So, tell me about you, Mackenzie. Are you married? Got any kids?"

Instead of answering his question, Mackenzie slipped behind the wheel of the car. "Listen—I wish I could spend more time catching up, but I've really gotta go."

"No problem," Dylan said easily, his hands resting on the door frame so he could close the door for her. "We're bound to run into each other again."

Mackenzie sent him a fleeting smile while she cranked the engine and shifted into gear. Fate had unexpectedly forced her hand and now she was just going to have to figure out how to deal with it.

## Chapter Two

Once out of Dylan's neighborhood, Mackenzie drove to the nearest public parking lot. She pulled into an empty space away from the other cars, fished her cell phone out of her pocket and dialed her best friend's number with shaky fingers.

"Rayna…?"

"Mackenzie? What's wrong? Why do you sound like that? Did something happen to Hope?"

"No." Mackenzie slouched against the door. "She's fine."

"Then what's wrong? You sound like something's wrong."

"I just ran into Dylan." There was a tremor in her voice.

"Dylan who?"

"What do you mean, Dylan *who*?" Mackenzie asked, irritated. "Dylan *Axel*."

"What?" Now she had Rayna's attention. "You're kidding!"

"No." Mackenzie rubbed her temple. She could feel a migraine coming on. "I'm *not* kidding."

"Where in the world did you run into him?"

"At his condo. In Mission Beach."

"He lives in Mission Beach?"

"Apparently so."

"What were you doing there?"

"Delivering cupcakes to Jordan's fiancé's birthday party," Mackenzie said as she tilted her head back and closed her eyes. "Dylan is *Ian's* best friend."

Rayna didn't respond immediately. After a few silent seconds, her friend said, "Oh. Wow. Are you okay?"

"I feel like I'm suffocating."

"Anxiety," Rayna surmised.

"Probably." Mackenzie put her free hand over her rapidly beating heart.

"Just close your eyes and take in long, deep breaths. You'll feel better in a minute."

"Okay…"

"Where are you now?"

"I'm parked. I didn't feel…stable enough to drive."

"That was smart," Rayna said. "Look—just take your time, pull yourself together and then come over. We'll figure this out. Hope's still at the barn?"

"Yeah. I pick her up at seven, after they bed down the horses."

"Charlie'll be home by the time you get here—we'll commiserate over pasta," Rayna said in her typical take-charge tone.

"Thank you." Comfort food with friends sounded like a great idea.

"And, Mackenzie?"

"Yeah?"

"It's going to be okay," Rayna said. "God is answering our prayers."

Rayna was one of the pastors for her nondenominational church of like-minded hippies and saw all life's events through the lens of a true believer.

"Hope's prayers," Mackenzie clarified. "Hope's prayers."

"Hope's prayers *are* our prayers. Aren't they?" Rayna countered gently. "Listen—I'll put on a pot of coffee and I'll see you when you get here. Be safe."

Mackenzie hung up the phone but didn't crank the engine immediately. Her mind was racing but her body was motionless. After ten minutes of taking long, deep breaths, Mackenzie finally felt calm enough to drive and set off for her friend's Balboa Park bungalow. Rayna was right. Her daughter's prayers *were* her prayers. She just hadn't been prepared for *this* prayer to be answered so quickly.

"Little one!" Molita Jean-Baptiste, the bakery manager, poked her head into the kitchen. "There's a young man out here who wants to talk to you."

"Okay," Mackenzie said as she slid a large pan of carrot-cake cupcakes into the oven. "I'll be right there."

Mackenzie closed the door of the industrial baking oven and then wiped her hands on a towel before she headed for the front of the bakery. She put a welcoming, professional smile on her face as she pushed the swinging doors apart and walked through. But her smile dropped for a split second when she saw Dylan standing next to one of the display counters.

"Hi," Dylan greeted her with his friendly, boyish smile. "Nice place."

"Thank you." Mackenzie glanced over at Molita who was restocking the cases and pretending to mind her own business. "Are you here to order cupcakes?"

"No." Dylan laughed. "I'm here to see you."

"Oh." Mackenzie frowned. "Okay."

For the last week, she had lost countless hours of sleep trying to figure out what to do about Dylan. And after so many sleepless nights, she *still* hadn't figured out how to blindside the man with a ten-year-old daughter.

"Would you like something to eat, young man?" Molita asked. Haitian-born and in her sixties now, Molita was as round as she was tall. Whether Molita was having a day of aches and pains or not, she always greeted the customers like family. She was the backbone of Nothin' But Cupcakes, and Mackenzie often joked that customers came to see Molita as much as they came for the cupcakes.

"No, thank you." Dylan put his hand on his flat stomach. "I'm trying to watch my girlish figure."

"Well…" Molita smiled warmly at Dylan. "You'll let me know if you change your mind. I just put on a fresh pot of coffee."

Dylan thanked Molita for the offer and then asked in a lowered voice, "Is there someplace we can talk?"

"Um…yeah. We can talk in my office, I suppose. But I only have a minute."

"This won't take too long," Dylan said.

"I'll be right back, Moll. I'm just going to step into my office for a minute or two."

"You know I'll call ya if I need'ja," Molita called out from behind the counter.

Dylan followed her to the office. She didn't typically take anyone to the office, and it struck her, when she opened the door, just how tiny and cluttered it really was.

"Sorry about the mess." Mackenzie shuffled some papers around in a halfhearted attempt to straighten up. "Believe it or not, I have a system in here…"

"I'm not worried about it." Dylan closed the door behind

him. If Jenna didn't use a coaster under a glass, it bugged him. But, for whatever reason, Mackenzie's untidy office didn't bother him so much.

Dylan squeezed himself into the small chair wedged in the corner on the other side of Mackenzie's desk.

"It smells really good in here." Dylan shifted uncomfortably, his knees pressed against the back of the desk.

Mackenzie hastily shoved some papers in a drawer. "Does it?"

"It does." Dylan looked around the office. "Now I know why you smell like a sugar cookie."

Surprised, Mackenzie slammed the drawer shut and stopped avoiding the inevitable eye contact with Dylan.

When Mackenzie looked at him with those unusual lavender-blue eyes, Dylan felt an unfamiliar tingling sensation in the pit of his stomach. There was something about Mackenzie's eyes that captivated him. He hadn't been able to get those eyes out of his head since the party.

"So…" Mackenzie said after an awkward lull. "What can I do for you, Dylan?"

Out of the corner of her eye, she could see the framed picture of her daughter, Hope, and resisted the urge to turn it away from Dylan.

"Actually…" Dylan tried to cross one leg over the other in the tight space and failed. "I wanted to do something for you."

Mackenzie pushed her long sleeves up to her elbows. "What's that?"

Dylan took the picture of Hope off the desk. "Cute kid. Yours?"

"Yes." Mackenzie's pulse jumped. "That's my daughter, Hope, at her fourth birthday party."

Mackenzie waited, anxiety twisting her gut, and wondered if Dylan would recognize his own flesh and blood in that picture. When he didn't, part of her was relieved and the other part was disappointed. Dylan put the picture back on the shelf without ever realizing that Hope was his. Mackenzie moved the frame to her side of the desk and turned it away from Dylan.

"Is Brand your married name? I remember you as Bronson." Dylan glanced down at the ring finger of her left hand.

"No." Mackenzie shook her head. "I decided to take my mom's maiden name when Hope was born. I wanted Hope to truly be her namesake."

Dylan's gaze was direct as he asked, "So, you're not married...?"

"No." Mackenzie wasn't subtle about looking up at the clock on the wall. As much as she knew that she needed to talk to Dylan about Hope, this wasn't the right time. They had three catering gigs set for the evening, and the afternoon lunch crowd would be lining up soon. She was already struggling to make payroll; she couldn't afford to lose one sale.

"Dylan...look, I don't mean to be rude..." Mackenzie started to say.

Dylan held up his hands and smiled sheepishly. "Okay... okay. I'll admit it. I'm stalling. It's just that, what I wanted to say to you seemed like a good idea this morning, but now..."

Mackenzie leaned forward on her arms and waited for Dylan to continue. Whatever it was that he wanted to say was making him turn red in the face and shift nervously in his chair. He had turned out to be a nice-looking man, with his dark brown hair and vivid green eyes. But Dylan wasn't classically handsome. He wasn't a pretty boy. Dylan's nose had been broken when they were kids and it hadn't healed back completely straight. There was a Y-shaped scar directly under his left eye from the time he'd caught a base-ball with his face during a Little League game. These little imperfections didn't detract from his good looks for Mackenzie; they enhanced them.

"All right." Dylan rubbed the back of his neck. "I'm just going to say what I came here to say. I owe you an apology, Mackenzie."

Mackenzie's chair squeaked loudly when she sat back. "Why in the world would you need to apologize to *me*?"

"Because..." Dylan looked at her directly in the eyes. "I remember what happened between us the night of Jett's wedding."

Mackenzie ran her hand over her leg beneath the desk and gripped her knee hard with her fingers. "Oh."

"Obviously that wasn't the sort of thing that I wanted to bring up while we were standing on the street."

"No." Mackenzie shook her head first and then nodded in agreement. "I'm glad you didn't."

"But...I didn't want you to think that I had forgotten about...*after* the reception..."

"We both had a lot to drink that night..." Mackenzie said faintly.

"Yes—we did. But, I still think I owe you an apology..." Dylan leaned forward. "You were Jett's little sister, and no matter how much I had to drink that night, I shouldn't have...taken advantage of you."

"Taken *advantage* of me?" Mackenzie asked incredu-lously. "You didn't take advantage of me, Dylan. I knew exactly what I was doing."

"You had just broken up with your boyfriend..." Dylan said.

"And you had just broken off your engagement..." Mackenzie countered. "I think we both need to just give each other a break about that night, okay?"

Dylan took a deep breath in as he thought about her words. Then he said, his expression pensive, "I should've called you, Mackenzie. After that night, I should've called you."

"And said what?"

"I don't know…" Dylan shrugged his shoulders. "I could've checked on you, made sure you were okay." He looked down at his hands for a second before he looked back up at her. "I should've let you know that I'd gotten back with Christa. I look back and I think maybe I used to be kind of an insensitive jerk…I know I can't apologize to everyone, but at least I have a chance to apologize to you."

"Well…" Mackenzie crossed her arms in front of her body. "I appreciate the apology, Dylan. I do. But, I never thought that you'd *wronged* me in any way. And I don't ever remember you being a jerk, at least not to me. You were the only one of my brother's friends who never ignored me. You never treated me like the weird *fat* girl."

"I never saw you that way," Dylan said, surprised. "And it'd make me feel better if you'd accept my apology…"

"Then I accept." It felt as if she just might be laying the groundwork for him to accept *her* apology later. "Of course I accept."

"Good." Dylan smiled at her. "Thank you."

"You're welcome." Mackenzie stood up. "Listen—I'm sorry that it seems like I'm always cutting things short, but…"

"No. No. That's okay." Dylan's chair knocked into the wall when he stood up. "I'm holding you up from work. But before I take off, I really want to show you something outside. It'll only take a second, I promise. And, trust me. You're gonna want to see what I have to show you."

"Okay. But then I really need to get back to work. I have a ton of special orders to fill." Mackenzie walked through the door that Dylan held open for her. "And let me tell you, there's a seedy underbelly of sugar addicts in San Diego and they all start to line up for a lunchtime fix." Mackenzie stopped at the counter and checked on Molita. "Are you doing okay, Moll?"

"Don't you worry about me, now. I've got everything under control." Molita sprayed glass cleaner on the front of the display case. "You go handle your business."

"I'll be right back," Mackenzie said.

"I wanted to show you my baby." Dylan held open the bakery door for her. "My girlfriend doesn't understand old school, but I knew you'd appreciate her."

Mackenzie stepped onto the sidewalk, but halted in her tracks just outside the door. "Is that what I *think* it is?"

Dylan smiled triumphantly at her as he walked over to his car. "Didn't I tell you you'd want to see her?"

Mackenzie couldn't take her eyes off Dylan's rare, vintage car. This car could easily sell for one hundred and fifty *thousand* dollars. "You do know that this is the stuff of legends, right?"

"You know I do," Dylan said. "And *you* know exactly what you're looking at, don't you?"

"Of course I do. I took Old School 101 with Dad and Jett…which I aced, by the way," Mackenzie bragged as she walked over to his car. "This sweet girl is a 1963 split-back Chevy Corvette. Super rare because the split window went out of production in 1964."

"You got it." Dylan's smile broadened.

"Basically, the Holy Grail." Mackenzie ran her hand along the curved hood of the car.

"That's right." Dylan nodded his head, his arms crossed loosely in front of him. "See? I *knew* you'd be excited to see her."

"You have no idea." Mackenzie walked around to the

back of the car. "Dylan—this's all original. Jett would die to get his hands on this car. She's not for sale, is she?"

"Not a chance." Dylan shook his head as he walked up to stand beside her. "But I really want Jett to restore my Charger."

Mackenzie found herself smiling at Dylan. "That would mean a lot to Jett, Dylan. It really would."

"I was thinking about giving the Charger this same silver-flake paint job with flat black accents. What do you think?"

Mackenzie's phone rang. "Hold that thought."

"Sure." Dylan leaned casually against his car.

"Hi, Aggie." Mackenzie leaned her head down and plugged one ear. "Wait a minute—what happened?" Mackenzie's face turned pale. "Tell Hope I'm on my way."

"Everything okay?" Dylan asked.

"No." Mackenzie headed back to the bakery. "My daughter got hurt at the barn."

"I hope she's okay," Dylan called after her.

"Thanks." Mackenzie pulled the bakery door open. Inside the bakery now, she stopped and threw up her hands in the air. "Tamara has my car! Molly—did you drive today?"

"My granddaughter dropped me off." Molita put a cupcake in a box for a customer.

Mackenzie made a quick U-turn and pushed the bakery door back open. "Molly—I have to go get Hope. Hold down the fort, okay?"

"What happened?" Molly asked, concerned.

"She hit her head at the barn." Mackenzie pushed the door open. "I'll call you later with an update as soon as I have one!"

Dylan had his blinker on and he was about to ease out onto the street when he saw Mackenzie bolt out of the cupcake shop and run toward his car. He braked and rolled down the passenger window.

Mackenzie bent down so she could see Dylan. "Can you give me a ride? My car is out with the deliveries."

Dylan reached over, unlocked the door and opened it for Mackenzie. "Hop in."

The thirty-minute ride out to the barn was a quiet one. Mackenzie's entire body was tense, her brow wrinkled with worry; seemingly lost in her own internal dialogue, she only spoke to give him directions. And he didn't press her for conversation. He imagined that if he were in her shoes, he wouldn't be in the mood for small talk, either.

"Turn left right here." Mackenzie pointed to a dirt side road up ahead. "You'll have to go slow in this car—with all the rain lately, there are potholes galore on the way to . the barn. Not many Corvettes brave this road."

"I can see why not." Dylan slowed way down as he turned onto the muddy dirt road. He looked at the large sign at the entrance of the road.

"Pegasus Therapeutic Riding—is that where we're heading?"

"Yes." Mackenzie unbuckled her seat belt.

Dylan glanced over at Mackenzie. "What's wrong with your daughter?"

"There's *nothing* wrong with Hope. She's perfect," Mackenzie snapped. After a second, she added in a tempered tone, "Hope loves horses and she loves helping people. Volunteering here is what she wants to do with her free time."

"She must take after you." Dylan drove up onto the grassy berm in order to avoid a large pothole. "I remember you were always busy with a cause…collecting canned goods and clothing for the homeless, volunteering at the animal shelter…you were never satisfied with playing video games and hanging out at the beach like the rest of us…"

Mackenzie's shoulders stiffened. She had been picked on mercilessly when she was a kid about her causes. "There's nothing wrong with caring about your community."

Dylan jerked the wheel to the left to avoid another pothole. He glanced quickly at Mackenzie; her arms were crossed, her jaw was clenched. He'd managed to put her on the defensive in record time. Usually he was pretty good at navigating his way around women.

"I meant it as a compliment," Dylan clarified. "And Hope sounds like a really good kid."

"She is." Mackenzie stared straight ahead. "She's the best kind of kid."

"How old did you say she was?"

"I didn't say." Mackenzie spotted the weathered brown barn up ahead. "You can pull in right there between the van and the truck…"

As Dylan eased the car to a stop, Mackenzie already had her hand on the door handle. With her free hand, she touched his arm briefly. "Thank you, Dylan. You've managed to rescue me twice in one week."

"Do you want me to wait here for you?" Dylan shifted into park.

"No!" Mackenzie pushed the door open and climbed out of the low-slung car. "I mean…no. That's okay. You've already done enough."

Dylan leaned down so he could see her face. "Are you sure?"

"Yes. Really. We'll be fine." Mackenzie closed the car door and hoped that she had also closed the subject of Dylan sticking around. Now that she was at the barn, she couldn't imagine what she had been thinking. This was *not* the time or place for Dylan to meet his daughter. Something that life-altering took planning. And she didn't have a plan. Not for this.

Dylan shut off the engine, pulled the keys out of the ignition and jumped out of the car. He wanted to follow Mackenzie, but she was sending out some pretty obvious back-off signals.

"I could just hang right here…."

Mackenzie spun around and walked backward a couple of steps. "I'll catch a ride from someone here. Really. I'm sure you have a day."

Dylan stared after Mackenzie. It didn't seem right just to drop her off and then leave, no matter what she said. But, on the other hand, she hadn't exactly been diplomatic about telling him to shove off. Reluctantly, Dylan climbed back into his car and shut the door. He rolled down the window, slipped the key in the ignition and turned the engine over. Mackenzie had been right about one thing. He did have a day. And he needed to get back to it.

## Chapter Three

Dylan shifted into Reverse, but he just couldn't bring himself to back out. Instead, he shifted back into Park, shut off the engine and got out of the car. Whether or not Mackenzie wanted him to make certain she was okay before he took off, it was something he felt he needed to do. Dylan set off toward the barn entrance; he carefully picked his way through long grass, weeds and sun-dried horse manure.

"You need some help?" Dylan was greeted by a young man in his early twenties leading a dark brown mare to one of the pastures. The young man appeared to have cerebral palsy and walked with a jerky, unsteady gate.

"I'm looking for Hope and her mom," Dylan said.

"They're in the office." The young man pointed behind him.

"Thanks," Dylan said just before he felt his left shoe sink into a fresh pile of manure. "Crap!"

"Yes, sir." The young man laughed as he turned the mare loose in the pasture. "That's exactly what it is."

Dylan shook his head as he tried to wipe the manure off his shoe in the grass. Today of all days he had to put on his Testoni lace-ups; he had spent some time this morning, polishing and buffing them to just the right amount of shine. Once he managed to semiclean his pricey leather shoes, he got himself back on track and found his way to the office. Dylan quietly stepped inside the disheveled hub of Pegasus. Dirt and hay were strewn across the floor and a large, rusty fan was kicking up more dust than circulating air. Mackenzie, a girl who must have been her daughter and a tall woman with cropped snow-white hair were gathered near a gray metal desk at the back of the rectangular office.

"Mom—I'm okay. When I bent down to grab a currycomb, I hit my head on the shelf. It's no big deal," Dylan heard Hope say.

Mackenzie brushed the girl's bangs out of the way to look at the bump on Hope's forehead. "Well—you've got a pretty good knot up there, kiddo."

"Here." The older woman held out a Ziploc baggy full of ice. "This'll hold her till you can get her checked out."

"But we still have more riders coming," Hope protested.

Mackenzie took the bag of ice. "Thanks, Aggie."

"They need my help, Mom! I'm *fine*. Really. I don't need to go to the doctor." Hope tried once again to reverse her fortune.

"Honey—I'm sorry." Mackenzie held her daughter's hand in hers. "We've gotta get this checked out. If the doctor gives you the green light, I promise, you'll be right back here tomorrow."

Hope sighed dramatically and pressed the ice to the lump on her forehead. "Fine."

Not wanting to interrupt the mother-daughter negotiation, Dylan hung back.

"Can I help you?" Aggie was suddenly in his face and confronting him like a protective mama bear with a cub.

Dylan slipped off his sunglasses and hooked them into the collar of his shirt. "I'm just checking on Mackenzie."

Mackenzie jerked her head around when she heard his voice. She swayed slightly and heard ringing in her ears as sheer panic sent her blood pressure soaring. "Dylan... why are you still here?"

"I'm just making sure you're okay before I leave." Dylan couldn't figure out why Mackenzie was freaked out about him looking out for her. Her overreaction struck him as odd.

Trapped, Mackenzie turned to face Dylan and blocked his view of Hope with her body. "That's my ride, Aggie."

"Oh!" Aggie wiped the sweat from the deep wrinkles etched into her brow. "If I'd known that, I would've made it a point to more cordial. I thought you might be one of them developers the Cook family's been sending around here lately...."

"Developers?" Mackenzie asked, temporarily distracted from her immediate problem.

Aggie waved her hand back and forth impatiently. "I don't want to borrow trouble talkin' about it right now.

"Agnes Abbot." Agnes stuck out her hand to Dylan. "You can call me Aggie or Mrs. Abbot—take your pick. But if you call me Agnes, don't expect an answer."

"Nice to meet you, Mrs. Abbot." Aggie's hand was damp and gritty. "Dylan Axel."

"And when I said that you could take your pick, I meant for you to pick Aggie."

"Aggie," Dylan repeated with a nod.

"Who's that, Mom?" Hope peeked around Mackenzie's body.

Realizing that there was no way out of this trap except forward, Mackenzie suddenly felt completely, abnormally, calm. This *was* going to happen. This meeting between father and daughter was unfolding organically, out of her control. Wasn't Rayna always preaching about life providing the right experiences at the right time? Maybe she was right. Perhaps she just needed to get out of life's way. So she did. She took a small step to the side and let Hope see her father for the first time.

"Hope—this is my friend Dylan." Her voice was surprisingly steady. "Dylan—I'd like you to meet my daughter, Hope."

Mackenzie zoomed in on Dylan's face first, and then Hope's, as they spoke to each other for the first time. If she had expected them to recognize each other instantly, like a made-for-TV movie, they didn't.

"Hi, Hope. How's your head?" Dylan had walked over to where Hope was sitting. For Mackenzie, it was so easy to see Dylan in Hope—the way she walked, the way she held her shoulders. Her smile.

"It doesn't even hurt," Hope explained to him.

Hope had Mackenzie's curly russet hair, cut into a bob just below her chin, as well as her mother's violet-blue eyes. But, that's where the resemblance ended. Her face was round instead of heart-shaped like her mother's; her skin was fairer and she had freckles on her arms and her face. The thought popped into his head that Hope must take strongly after her father's side of the family.

To Aggie, Hope said, "I think I should stay here. Don't you think I should stay?"

"No, ma'am." Aggie shook her head while she riffled around in one of the desk's drawers. "Your mom's got the right idea. They'll be just fine without us while we get you checked out."

"Nice try, kiddo." Mackenzie held out her hand to Hope. "You're going."

*"Man..."* Hope's mouth drooped in disappointment. But she put her hand into Mackenzie's hand and stood up slowly.

"Come on, kiddo…cheer up." Mackenzie wrapped her arm tightly around Hope's shoulders and kissed the top of her head. "We've been through worse, right?"

"Right." Hope gave her mom a halfhearted smile and returned the hug.

"Found one." Aggie pulled a pamphlet out of the pencil drawer and tromped over to Dylan in her knee-high rubber boots.

"Here." Aggie pressed the pamphlet into Dylan's hand, then she tapped on the front of it. "Here's the 411 on this place. We're always looking for volunteers. Do you have any horse experience?"

Dylan looked at the pamphlet. "Actually, I do."

"Perfect! We can always use another volunteer with some horse sense," Aggie said to him, hands resting on her squared hips. Then to Mackenzie, she said, "Well—let's get."

While Dylan skimmed the pamphlet quickly, it occurred to Mackenzie that she had just survived a moment that she had dreaded, and worried herself sick about, for years. Dylan and Hope had met and the world hadn't fallen off its axis. It gave her reason to believe that when the truth about their relationship came out, things would be okay for all of them.

Dylan folded the pamphlet and tucked it into his front pocket.

"Are you going to volunteer?" Hope asked him.

Mackenzie and Hope were standing directly in front of him now, arm in arm, the close bond between mother and daughter on display. It didn't surprise him that Mackenzie had turned out to be a dedicated and attentive mother. The way she had always taken care of every living thing around her when they were young, he didn't doubt it had been an easy transition into motherhood.

"I don't know." Dylan shifted his eyes between mother and daughter. "Maybe."

"You should." Hope tucked some of her hair behind her ear. "It's really fun."

From the doorway, Aggie rattled her keys. "We're burning daylight here! Let's go!"

"We're coming," Mackenzie said to Aggie, then to Dylan, "Thank you, Dylan. I'm sure you had a lot of things to do today. I hope this didn't put you behind schedule too much…"

"I was glad I could help." Dylan found himself intrigued, once again, by Mackenzie's unique lavender-blue eyes.

"Well…thank you again." Mackenzie sent him a brief smile. "Come on, kiddo. Aggie's already got the truck running."

"Nice to meet you, Hope," Dylan said.

"Bye." Hope lifted her hand up and gave a short wave.

Dylan waited for Mackenzie and Hope to turn and head toward the door. As Hope turned, something on the very top of her left ear caught his eye. Instead of following directly behind them, Dylan was too distracted to move. Dylan's eyes narrowed and latched on to Hope as he reached up to touch a similar small bump at the top of his own left ear.

"Are you coming, Dylan?" Mackenzie had paused in the doorway.

"What?" Dylan asked, distracted.

"Are you coming?" Mackenzie repeated.

Dylan swallowed hard several times. He couldn't seem to get his mouth to move, so he just nodded his response and forced himself to remain calm. Hands jammed into his front pockets, Dylan followed them out. He watched as Mackenzie and Hope piled into Aggie's blue long-bed dual-tire truck. Aggie backed out, Mackenzie waved goodbye and Dylan's jumbled thoughts managed to land on one very disturbing truth: the only other time he had ever seen a small bump like Hope's was when he was looking at himself in the mirror.

Instead of heading to the studio, which was his original plan, Dylan drove home on autopilot from the barn. His mind was churning like a hamster on a hamster wheel, just going around and around in the same circle. No matter how hard he tried, he couldn't remember if he'd used a condom when he'd slept with Mackenzie. He had always been religious about it, but he hadn't expected to sleep with anyone at the wedding. He had still been licking his wounds from his breakup with Christa, and ending up in Mackenzie's hotel room that night had been a completely unplanned event. And, unless Mackenzie was in the habit of carrying condoms, which seemed out of character, there was a real good chance they'd had unprotected sex that night. In that case, it was possible, *highly* possible that Mackenzie's daughter was his child.

Dylan pulled into the garage and parked next to his black Viper. He jumped out of his car and headed inside. He walked straight into the downstairs bathroom, flipped on the light and leaned in toward the mirror. He touched the tiny bump on his ear with his finger. He hadn't been imagining it—Hope's bump matched his. What were the odds that another man, the one who'd fathered Hope, would have the same genetic mark?

"I wouldn't bet on it," Dylan said as he left the bathroom. He went into the living room and pulled open the doors of the custom-built bookcases. He knelt down and started to search through the books on the bottom shelf. He found what he was looking for and pulled it off the shelf. His heart started to thud heavily in his chest as he sat down in his recliner and opened the old family photo album. On the way home, an odd thought had taken root in his mind. There was something so familiar about Hope and he couldn't get a particular family photo, one of his favorites, out of his mind.

Dylan flipped through the pages of the album until he found the photo he'd been looking for. He turned on the light beside the recliner and held the photo under the light.

"No…" Dylan leaned over and studied the photo of his mother and his aunt Gerri sitting together on the porch. His mom had to be around twelve and Aunt Gerri looked to be near eight or nine. Hope was the spitting image of Aunt Gerri. Yes, she had Mackenzie's coloring, but those features belonged to *his* family. That bump on Hope's ear came directly from *his* genes. He'd stake his life on it.

*"No…"* Dylan closed his eyes. A rush of heat crashed over his body, followed by a wave of nausea. He had a daughter. He was a father. Hope was *his* child.

*What the hell is going on here?*

"Babe!" Jenna came through the front door carrying an empty tote bag over her shoulder. "Where are you?"

"In the den." Dylan leaned forward and dropped his head down.

"There you are…" Jenna dropped her bag on the floor. She climbed into his lap and kissed him passionately on the mouth.

"I've missed you, babe." Jenna curled her long legs up; rested her head on his shoulder.

"I've missed you, too," Dylan said in a monotone.

"Whatcha lookin' at?" Jenna asked.

Dylan reached over with his free hand and shut the album. "I was just checking something out for Aunt Gerri."

"Be honest." Jenna unbuttoned the top button of his shirt. "Are you upset with me?"

"Why would I be upset with you?" Dylan felt suffocated and wished Jenna wasn't sitting on him, but he didn't have the heart to push her away.

"Because I'm going to be staying with Denise in LA… didn't you get my message?"

Dylan tried to focus on what Jenna was saying. "When are you leaving?"

"Tomorrow. Remember the audition I had this week? I got the pilot!" Jenna squealed loudly as she hugged him tightly. "Can you believe it?!"

"Congratulations, Jenna. I'm really happy for you."

"And not mad?"

"No." Dylan rubbed his hand over her arm. "Of course not."

"I mean—we can still probably see each other on weekends."

"Sure."

"And…" Jenna kissed the side of his neck. "I think the sex'll be even hotter when we *do* see each other, don't you think?"

Dylan tried to muster a smile in response, but he just wanted her to get off his lap.

"Do you want to go upstairs for a quickie before I grab my stuff?" Jenna slipped her hand into his shirt so she could run her hand over his bare chest. "I only have, like, an hour because I have to finish packing over at my place, but…we still have time. If you want…"

Dylan patted her leg. "Not now, Jenna. I'm…beat."

Jenna shrugged nonchalantly. "That's okay. But at least come up and keep me company while I pack."

Jenna uncurled herself from his lap, held out her hand and wiggled her fingers so he'd take her hand. Dylan followed Jenna up the stairs. He sat on the edge of the soaker tub while Jenna cleaned out the drawer he had cleared out for her. He listened while she chattered excitedly about her new job, but he couldn't focus on her words. His mind was fixated on one thing and one thing only: Hope. Usually he enjoyed hanging out with low-demand Jenna. But today she was grating on his nerves, and he had never been so happy to see her go. He had gone through the motions of carrying her bag out to her BMW and then kissing her as if he meant it before she drove away. There was an unspoken goodbye in that kiss; he had the feeling that it was only a matter of time before their relationship fizzled under the pressure of distance. They had both always known that neither one of them was playing a long game.

After seeing the last of her taillights, Dylan closed the front door and went outside on the balcony so he could look at the ocean waves. He needed to clear his head, figure out his next move. The best way he knew to clear his head was to get on his surfboard. The waves were small, but he didn't care. He just needed to blow off some steam and get his head screwed back on straight. After he spent several hours pounding the waves, Dylan jumped into the shower with clarity of mind—he knew exactly what he needed to do. He wasn't about to let this thing fester overnight. He was going to have to confront Mackenzie. He was going to ask her point-blank if Hope was his child. *Direct* was the only way he knew how to do business. Dylan dried off quickly, pulled on some casual clothes and then dialed a familiar number.

"Jordan. I'm glad I caught you." Dylan held a pen in his hand poised above a pad of paper. "Listen—I think I may have a job for your cousin Mackenzie. Can I grab her number from you real quick?"

Mackenzie put all of Hope's medicine bottles back in the cabinet. Even though Hope had fought it valiantly, getting injured at the barn, however minor, had worn her out. After she ate and took her medicine, Hope had gone to bed early.

"So tell me what happened," Rayna said over the phone. "They actually met today?"

Mackenzie pushed some recipe boxes out of the way and sat down on the love seat. "I needed a ride. He was there. It just happened."

"Well…you know I don't believe in coincidences…"

"I know…"

"So…what are you going to do?"

Mackenzie slumped down farther into the cushion and rubbed her eyes. "I'm going to get myself through this week, and then I'm going to call him. Ask to meet."

"I think you're doing the right thing. Do you know what you're going to say?"

"No. Not a clue." Mackenzie stared up at the ceiling. "I have a couple of days to think about it. What's the etiquette on something like this?"

"I don't know. We could look it up online."

Mackenzie kicked off her shoes and pulled off her socks. "I was joking, Ray."

"I know. But I bet there's a ton of stuff out there about how you tell your baby daddy that he *is* your baby daddy…"

Mackenzie curled into the fetal position on the love seat. "Ugh. I hate that term. *Baby daddy.*"

"Sorry. But you know what I mean. You know someone had to write a 'how to' manual. There's probably a *DNA for Dummies* out there…"

Mackenzie's phone chirped in her ear, signaling call waiting. "Hold on, Ray. Someone's calling."

Mackenzie took the phone away from her ear and looked at the incoming call.

*Dylan Axel* was the name that flashed across the screen.

"Dylan's on the other line," Mackenzie told Ray.

"I'm hanging up," Rayna said quickly. "Call me back!"

Dylan couldn't sit still while he waited for Mackenzie to answer. He had been staring at Mackenzie's number for nearly an hour. Before he dialed her number, he began to question his own logic. Yet, after nearly an hour of careful consideration, his gut just wouldn't stop prodding him to place the call. If Hope *was* his daughter, then he had a right to know.

"Hello?" Mackenzie picked up the line.

"It's Dylan, Mackenzie." It was work to control his tone. "How's Hope?"

"She's worn out, but doing fine. The doctor cleared her to return to the barn tomorrow…"

"I'm glad to hear it." Dylan was pacing in a circular pattern.

After an uncomfortable silence, Mackenzie asked, "Um…did Jordan give you my private number?"

"Yes." Dylan needed to get to the point. "She did. Look—there's something that I need to ask you, Mackenzie."

There was a razor-sharp edge in Dylan's tone that brought her to the edge of the love seat.

"What's that?" Her attempt to sound casual failed.

"And I need you to give me an honest answer…"

Dylan stopped pacing, closed his eyes and tried to control his out-of-control heartbeat, as he posed his simple, straightforward question:

"Is Hope my child?"

## *Chapter Four*

Mackenzie sat like a statue on the edge of the love seat, but bit her lip so hard that she could taste blood on her tongue. Once again, fate had snatched control away from her grasp. She had wanted to broach the subject with Dylan gently, calmly, at the right moment and in the right setting. This wasn't how she wanted it to go at all.

Dylan waited impatiently at the other end of the line. But he had heard Mackenzie suck in her breath when he asked the question, followed by silence. For him, he already had his answer. Hope was his daughter.

"Mackenzie." Dylan repeated the question, "Is Hope my child?"

Mackenzie stared in the direction of Hope's room, grateful that she had gone to bed early. "I…" She whispered into the phone, "I don't think that we should discuss this over the phone."

"You're probably right," Dylan agreed. "You pick the place and time and I'll be there."

"I can meet after work tomorrow." Mackenzie pushed herself to a stand. "But I don't know where we should meet."

"Let's meet at my place." Dylan's forehead was in his hand, his eyes squeezed tightly shut.

Mackenzie pressed her back against the wall and crossed one arm tightly over her midsection. "I'll get my friends to watch Hope. I can be at your place around six-fifteen, six-thirty."

"I'll see you then." Dylan opened his eyes. "Good night, Mackenzie."

"Good night." Mackenzie touched the end button and slowly slid down the wall until she was sitting on the floor. She wrapped her arms tightly around her legs and rested her forehead on her knees. From the moment she had held Hope in her arms at the hospital, she had *felt*, like a splinter under her skin, this day would eventually come. And now that it had, she felt undeniably shell-shocked and strangely...*relieved*.

But with the relief came another strain of uncertainty. She prayed for Hope's sake that Dylan wouldn't reject her. But what if Dylan decided that he wanted to play a larger role in Hope's life? She had raised Hope on her own for ten years. It had always been Mackenzie and Hope against the world. And she knew she was being selfish, but she *liked it* that way.

When Dylan ended the call, he started to straighten up the condo to keep his body busy and his mind occupied. He moved restlessly from room to room, cleaning surfaces and pounding pillows into submission. He wound up back in the kitchen and began to unload the dishwasher even though the housekeeper would be there in the morning. One by one, he put the glasses in the cabinet, setting them down hard and then shutting the cabinet doors a little bit more firmly than he normally would. Finished with the chore, Dylan tried to push the dishwasher drawer back in, but it caught.

"Dammit!" Dylan rattled it back into place and then with a hard shove, slammed it forward. He lifted up the dishwasher door and shut it, hard. Stony faced, he leaned back against the counter, arms crossed over his chest. Still frustrated and restless, Dylan headed down to the beach and once his feet hit the sand, he started to run. He was grateful for the cover of the night. He was grateful that there were only a few souls on the beach with him. He started to run faster, his feet pounding on the hard-packed sand. Pushing his body harder, pushing himself to go faster and farther than he had ever gone before. His lungs burned, but he didn't let up. His leg muscles burned, but he didn't let up. He didn't let up until his leg muscles gave way and he stumbled. His hands took the brunt of his body weight as he fell forward into the sand. Fighting to catch his breath, he sat back, and dropped his head down to his knees. He pressed his sandy fingers into his eyes and then pinched the side of his nose to stop tears from forming.

He'd never wanted to be a father and he'd worked damn hard to make sure it never happened. That he never had a slipup. He had been *vigilant* all of his sexual life to make sure that he never got anyone pregnant. Even if he had been dating someone for a while, even if he saw them take the pill every day, he *always* wore a condom. But the one time he didn't—the *one* time he *didn't*—he'd gotten caught. And now, he had to face the one fear he had never intended to face: Was being a bad father genetic?

"I'm here." Mackenzie pulled into a parking spot a couple of doors down from Dylan's condo. She was on speakerphone with Rayna and Charlie.

"Mackenzie—you've got this," Charlie said.

"And don't forget—" Rayna began.

"Rayna," Mackenzie interrupted her. "Please, please, *please* don't give me another spiritual affirmation. I just can't take it right now."

After a pause, Rayna said in her "let's meditate" voice, "I was just going to say—don't forget that we're always here for you, anytime, no matter what."

"Oh. Sorry. Thank you," Mackenzie said. "I'll be by to pick up Hope after I'm done."

Mackenzie hung up with her friends and then got out of the car. She stood by her car for several minutes, staring at Dylan's condo, before she forced herself to get the show on the road. Stalling wouldn't help. She needed to face this conversation with Dylan head-on and get it out of the way.

Mackenzie took a deep breath in and knocked on the door. This time, unlike the last time she stood in this spot, Dylan opened the door seconds after she knocked.

"Come on in." Dylan stepped back and opened the door wider.

Mackenzie walked, with crossed arms, through the door and into Dylan's world. She noticed, more so than she had the first time she was here, how neat and organized Dylan's home was. His home was sleek, expensive and masculine: the ultimate bachelor pad. It was a sharp contrast to her 1930s Spanish-style Balboa Park rental with an interior decor that was cobbled together with flea-market finds and garage-sale bargains. The lives they lived, the lives they had built for themselves, couldn't be more different.

"Can I get you something to drink?" Dylan stood several feet away from her, hands hidden in his front pockets. He looked different today. The boyish spark was gone from his eyes. The features of his face were hardened, his mouth unsmiling. Today, he seemed more like a man to her than he ever had before.

"No. Thank you." Mackenzie shook her head, wishing she were already on the back end of this conversation.

"Let's talk in the den." Dylan slipped his left hand out of his pocket and gestured for her to walk in front of him. "After you."

Mackenzie waited for Dylan to sit down before she said, "I'm not sure where to begin..."

"Why don't we start with an answer to my question." Dylan was determined not to let this conversation spiral out of control. He had always been known for his cool head and he wanted to keep it that way.

"I think you've already figured out the answer to your question, Dylan. But if you need to hear me say it, then I'll say it," Mackenzie said in a measured, even voice. "Hope is your daughter."

Instead of responding right away, Dylan stood up and walked over to the large window that overlooked the ocean. He stared out at the waves and rubbed his hand hard over his freshly shaven jawline. With a shake of his head, he turned his back to the window.

"I'm just trying to wrap my mind around this, Mackenzie. It's not every day that my friend's sister turns up with my kid."

"I understand." Mackenzie wished that she could stop the sick feeling of nerves brewing in her stomach.

"How long have you known that she's mine, Mackenzie?" Dylan asked pointedly. "Have you always known... or did you think that she was your ex-boyfriend's child?"

Mackenzie's stomach gurgled loudly. Embarrassed, she pressed her hands tightly into her belly. "I've always known."

"How?" Dylan asked quietly, his face pale. "How did you know?"

"You were the only one I'd slept with in months, Dylan. It couldn't've been anyone else *but* you."

Dylan leaned back against the window; he felt off balance. "That's not what I expected you to say."

"It's the truth…." Mackenzie said.

Dylan didn't respond; he didn't move. He didn't trust himself to speak, so he didn't.

"I have a question for you." Mackenzie turned her body toward him. "What made you think she was yours?"

"The bump…on her ear. It matches mine."

"Oh…" Mackenzie said faintly. Dylan had always worn his hair long when they were kids—she never noticed that birthmark before.

"And then there was this." Dylan retrieved the photo album, opened it and held it out for Mackenzie to take.

"Look familiar?" Dylan pointed to the picture of his aunt Gerri.

Mackenzie nodded, stared closely at the picture.

"Who needs a DNA test, right?" Dylan nodded toward the picture.

Mackenzie stared at the old black-and-white photograph. "This little girl…she's the spitting image of Hope." Mackenzie looked up. "Who is she?"

"That's my aunt Gerri when she was nine."

"I remember your aunt Gerri. We went to their horse farm a couple of times. She played the organ for us."

Dylan's jaw set. "Hope should be able to remember my aunt Gerri, too. Uncle Bill's the closest thing to a father I've ever had. He *deserved* the chance to know my daughter."

Dylan's well-crafted barb hit its intended mark. And it hurt. Because Mackenzie knew that he was right. Silently, she carefully closed the photo album and handed it back to Dylan.

Dylan put the photo album on the coffee table and sunk down on the couch a cushion away from Mackenzie. He leaned forward, rested his elbows on his legs and cradled his head in his hands.

"So…" Dylan said quietly. "We both know she's mine. The next question I'd like answered is…why did you know ten years ago and I'm only finding out *now*?"

Mackenzie leaned away from Dylan. "I found out I was pregnant really early on. I'm regular…like clockwork. So when I didn't get my period after the wedding…I knew."

"And you didn't think it was important to share this information with me, because…?"

"I was going to tell you. It never occurred to me *not* to tell you."

"But you didn't…" Dylan lifted his head, looked at her. "Why not?"

"Jett told me that you were back with Christa…"

"Jett knew?"

"No. Not back then. And not until long after the two of you had already lost touch."

Dylan nodded and Mackenzie continued her story.

"After I found out that your engagement was back on, I thought it was the best thing for both of us if I didn't tell you…"

"No." Dylan shook his head. "You should have told me. I had the *right* to know."

"You forget, Dylan. I knew how much you loved Christa. That's all you talked about the night Jett got married. And you and I both know what would've happened if she found out you'd gotten someone *pregnant* at the wedding! She would've broken off the engagement and you would have lost the love of your life because of me!

I couldn't see any *reason* to screw up your life, Dylan… not when *I* didn't even know if I wanted to keep the baby."

"I didn't *marry* Christa," Dylan challenged her. "But, you *did* keep the baby."

"Yes. I did. I thought about adoption. I thought about… abortion. In the end, I decided to keep her."

Dylan stabbed his leg with his finger. "That's a decision we should have made *together*."

"I admit that I may have called it wrong…"

"Called it wrong…?" he repeated incredulously.

"But I was young and I thought I was doing the right thing for all of us." Mackenzie touched her finger to her chest. "I got Hope and you got to marry the woman you loved."

"I didn't even know what love was back then…" Dylan shook his head. "At least now I know why you were so anxious to get rid of me at the barn the other day. You didn't want me to meet my own daughter."

"Not like that I didn't." Mackenzie set the record straight. "I didn't want that for Hope…and I didn't want that for you."

In a rough voice, Dylan asked, "Were you ever going to tell me, Mackenzie? Or were you just going to let me go the rest of my life not knowing?"

"No." Mackenzie clasped her hands together. "I was going to tell you. I had decided to start looking for you this year…"

Dylan's eyes were glassy with emotion. "You're telling me…that if we hadn't run into each other at Ian's party, you were going to track me down? Why? Why now*?*"

Mackenzie took a deep breath in and when she let it out, her shoulders sagged.

"It's what Hope wanted. When we were filling out her

Make-A-Wish application, she wrote—I wish I could meet my dad."

"Wait a minute…" What she had just said didn't sink into his head right away. "Make-A-Wish? Isn't that for sick kids?"

"Yes." Mackenzie waited for Dylan to ask the next logical question.

"Are you trying to tell me that Hope is sick?"

"Hope has been battling leukemia for the last two years." Mackenzie managed to say those words without tearing up.

As Dylan often did, he went silent. He stared at her for a long time with puzzled, narrowed eyes.

"Do you need a drink?" he finally asked. "I need a drink."

Dylan stood up suddenly and walked toward the kitchen. He stopped when he realized that she was still sitting on the couch. "Are you coming?"

Wordlessly, Mackenzie stood up on shaky legs and followed Dylan into the kitchen.

"Can I interest you in a cold malt beverage?" Dylan pulled a bottle of beer from the side door.

"Sure. Why not?"

"Why not, indeed," Dylan said cryptically as he popped the tops off the beers and handed her one. "We're both consenting adults here."

"Thank you," Mackenzie said. She brought the bottle up to her mouth but Dylan stopped her.

"What should we toast to?" He held out his bottle to her.

"Anything you'd like," Mackenzie said tiredly. She was exhausted. She was exhausted all the time, and had been for years. The stress of Hope's illness and the stress of trying to run a business had been catching up with her for a long time. And now she had a sinking feeling that dealing with Dylan was only going to add to her exhaustion.

Dylan tapped her bottle with his. "To Hope."

"To Hope," Mackenzie seconded.

"Could you go for some fresh air?" Dylan asked.

Mackenzie nodded and Dylan opened the French door leading out to the deck. "After you."

Mackenzie stepped onto the large deck and was immediately drawn to the edge of the railing that overlooked the beach. She stared at the sun setting over the small, rolling waves and tried to relax her shoulders. Dylan, who used to be so simple to read, wasn't so easy for her to read tonight. She had no idea what type of emotional shift she might encounter. Next to her, but not too close, Dylan rested his forearms on the railing, bottle loosely held in one hand.

"So…" Dylan said in a calm, almost contemplative tone. "Hope has cancer."

"Yes…" Mackenzie nodded. "She has acute lymphoblastic leukemia. ALL. She was diagnosed when she was eight."

"Leukemia. What is that? Blood cancer?"

Mackenzie nodded. "At first I just thought that she was pushing herself too hard between school and the barn. She was tired all the time, losing weight. She just wasn't herself. When she started to complain about an ache in her bones and a sore throat…" Mackenzie lifted one shoulder. "I thought she was coming down with the flu. I mean… who would immediately jump to cancer?"

Dylan sat down in one of the chairs encircling a fire pit. Mackenzie joined him.

"I remember being really stressed out that day…the day we found out. I had to rearrange my entire morning so I could get Hope to the doctor. Traffic was ridiculous, I was on the phone with the bakery…on the phone with clients…I remember thinking that it was the worst possible time for Hope to be catching something on top of everything else." Mackenzie pushed strands of hair out of her face. "And all I could do was start adding things to do to my already gigantic to-do list—stop by the pharmacy, arrange for someone to stay with Hope…blah, blah, blah…"

Mackenzie stopped to take a swig from her beer. She shook her head as she swallowed the liquid down. "I had no idea how frivolous *everything* I'd just been obsessing over was about to become."

Dylan listened intently, while Mackenzie talked. "The doctor sent us to the hospital, tests were run and she was diagnosed that day. And just like that…literally in what seemed like the blink of an eye…our world imploded. No parent is ever prepared to hear the words *your child has cancer.*" Mackenzie rubbed fresh tears out of her eyes. "But even more than that, I'll never forget the look on Hope's face when she asked me—'Did she just say that I have cancer?' I've never been that scared in my life. Hope was admitted to the hospital, and ever since then, our lives just became this never-ending revolving door of chemo and steroids and tests and checkups and hospital stays…"

When Mackenzie realized that she was the only one talking *and* that she had said much more than she had ever intended, she stopped herself from blurting out more by taking a swig of her now-tepid beer. She picked at the label on the bottle, wishing that Dylan would do something other than sit in his designer lounge chair and stare at her.

"I don't know why I just told you all of that," Mackenzie said to fill the silence.

At first, Dylan really didn't know what to say. He had been dragged from one emotional spectrum to the next in the span of an hour. At the beginning of their meeting, all he felt for Mackenzie was anger. But while Mackenzie was telling her story, and with the ocean wind blowing the wispy tendrils of her hair across her pretty face, she reminded him of the girl she had once been. The girl he remembered so vividly from his childhood—the chubby bookworm with thick glasses who used to read her books in the backseat of one of her father's vintage cars. All the boys in the neighborhood ignored Jett's sister, but he never did. Maybe it was because he liked how different she was than the rest of the girls. Or maybe it was because he had only seen her smile once after her mom died. He had never thought to analyze it. He had always just *liked* Mackenzie.

"Because we used to be friends," Dylan said.

"Were we?" Mackenzie asked.

"I always thought so." Dylan caught her gaze and held it. "And I tell you this, Mackenzie. If I had known that you were pregnant…if you had just trusted me enough to give me a chance, I never would've let you or Hope go through any of this stuff alone. I would have been there for you… both of you…every step of the way."

## Chapter Five

It took Dylan a couple of weeks to make a decision about Hope. He had gone about his daily life trying to focus on business. He hadn't told anyone about Hope, not his girlfriend, his aunt or his best friend. He needed to get right with it in his own head before he could open up to other people. And after many distracted days and restless nights, he had an epiphany of sorts: Didn't he have a moral obligation to Hope? Yes, the idea of becoming an "instant parent" terrified him. But if he was brutally honest with himself, the idea of repeating his father's mistakes scared him even more. Once he came to a decision, he took the only next logical step: he called Mackenzie.

"Hello?" Mackenzie answered the phone.

"Hi, Mackenzie. It's Dylan. How are you?"

"I'm fine. Busy. But fine," Mackenzie said. "Hope's doing really well. Her recent blood tests came back clear. She's still in remission."

"That's good to hear."

When he didn't add anything more, Mackenzie asked, "How are you doing, Dylan?"

"I'm okay. Still sorting through this thing, I think." Dylan rested his forehead in his hand. "Look, Mackenzie, I've been thinking a lot about Hope…are you sure that getting to know me is what your daughter wants?"

Mackenzie hated that she hesitated before she said, "I'm sure."

"Then, let's set it up." Dylan stared out the window at the calm ocean in the distance. His tone was steady but his heart was pounding.

"Um…" Mackenzie rubbed her temples to prevent a migraine from flaring up. "I haven't told Hope that I found you yet. I was waiting to hear from you. I didn't want to get her excited and then…well, you know…"

"Understood." Dylan sounded as if he was arranging a business meeting rather than a meeting with his newly discovered daughter. It was his comfort zone and it helped him stay sane. "When can you get that done?"

"Not tonight," Mackenzie said distractedly. "She has chemo tomorrow and she'll be sick all weekend…but maybe next week sometime when she's feeling better…"

"That's fine." Dylan nodded his head. "Once that's done, give me a call and we'll figure out the next step. Does that work for you?"

"Yes," Mackenzie said after she cleared her throat. "I'll call you once I've spoken with my daughter."

After they ended the call, Mackenzie stared at the phone for several seconds.

"Well?" Rayna was staring at her like a cat gearing up to pounce on a catnip toy. "That had to be Dylan, right? What did he *say*?"

"He wants to meet Hope."

Rayna turned the burner on the stove down. "See? Look at that! Prayers in action! This is *great* news!"

"What's great news?" Charlie walked through the front door wearing mint-green scrubs. She hung her keys on the hook just inside the door.

"Hi, honey." Rayna smiled at her wife, Charlotte. "Dylan finally came to his senses and called. He's agreed to meet Hope!"

Rayna was the yin to Charlotte's yang. Rayna had shoulder-length wispy blond hair, pretty, Slavic features and alabaster skin. Charlotte, who preferred to be called Charlie, was an attractive mix of Irish and Mexican heritage with light brown eyes, golden-chestnut skin and thick black wavy hair worn loose and long. At first, Rayna and Charlie were just her landlords, but they had become family after Hope was diagnosed. Rayna and Charlie had been in the trenches with them right from the start—cooking meals, running errands and pulling all-nighters watching Hope while Mackenzie caught a few hours of sleep. And Rayna's church had held fundraisers to help raise money to help pay for Hope's burgeoning medical bills. It was hard to imagine how she would have gotten through the first year of Hope's treatment without them.

"Huh…" Charlie kissed Rayna on the lips. "How come you're happy and Mackenzie's not?"

"You know Mackenzie resists change." Ray held out a wooden spoon to Charlie. "Here. Taste this."

Charlie tasted the sauce. "That's really good."

"I don't think I *resist* change," Mackenzie said.

A sleepy-eyed, rotund gray tabby cat named Max appeared. Charlie scooped him up, kissed him on the head. "I thought this was the call you've been waiting for all week…?"

"It's not that I'm *not* glad that he called. I am. It's just a lot to take in, that's all. It's always just been Hope and me." Mackenzie rested her chin on her hand. "I like how things are between us now…"

"Resistant to change," Rayna said in a singsong voice.

Charlie got some water and then joined Mackenzie at the kitchen table. "But maybe this will turn out to be a great thing. You yourself already said that he's a good guy. What could it hurt to have another person share the load? Between the bakery and managing Hope's leukemia treatments, let's face it…you've got your hands full."

At Mackenzie's feet, Max was preparing for a leap onto her lap. Mackenzie patted her legs for encouragement.

"Oh, my dear lord, what have you been feeding this cat, Ray?" Max landed on her leg with a grunt. "I thought he was on a diet."

Charlie sent Rayna an "I told you so" look. Rayna was immediately defensive. "He *is* on a diet! Don't listen to them, Max-a-million. You're just big boned!" Rayna pointed a spatula at her. "And don't change the subject. What's really scaring you?"

Rayna could read her like a book. "I don't know. I suppose I am, a little scared. I mean…what if…"

"What if…" Mackenzie hadn't admitted this private thought aloud. "What if Dylan ends up wanting custody of Hope? What if Hope decides that she wants to live with him down the road?"

Charlie and Rayna both shook their heads in unison.

"Nope. Not gonna happen." Charlie twisted her thick wavy hair into a bun.

Rayna came to the table. "Not a chance."

"I feel stupid admitting that out loud…" Mackenzie scratched behind Max's chops.

"It's not stupid," Rayna said. "It's human."

"I suppose so…" Mackenzie helped Max to the floor

safely. "You know what, guys? If it's all the same to you, I think I'm just gonna skip dinner."

"Are you sure?" Rayna asked, disappointed. "I was going to try out a new recipe on you! And I have wine…"

"Yeah. I'm sure." She stood up, glad that she lived next door. "I just need some time to…decompress before Hope gets back from the movies."

"Bath salts, candles and a hot bath." Rayna hugged her tightly at the door. "Everything always looks better after a bath."

Dylan drove slowly up the winding, tree-lined private driveway that led to his aunt's farm. When he was growing up, and Uncle Bill was still alive, the farm had been bustling with activity. Now the place felt lifeless. The horses were gone, the stable hands and horse trainers were gone. The only thing left were empty pastures, empty stables and Aunt Gerri's sprawling two-story 1900s farmhouse with its wraparound porch and old tin roof. At one time, Forrest Hanoverians claimed over a hundred acres and were renowned for the quality of their Hanoverian breeding program. Over the years, Aunt Gerri had sold off much of the farm's land until only the central twenty acres of the farm remained.

Dylan parked his car in the circle driveway in front of the house. Aunt Gerri swung open the front door and waved at him.

"I was just getting ready to play the organ, when I saw you coming up the driveway!" Aunt Gerri called to him from the door. Just shy of her eighty-third birthday, Geraldine Forrest was a petite woman with intelligent bright blue eyes, a steel-trap memory and a kind-hearted disposition. Dylan always marveled at her energy; she kept herself busy going to garage sales, playing the organ at her church and socializing with her long list of friends.

"How are you, Aunt Gerri?" Dylan walked up the porch steps.

"Well...I'll tell you...I'm fit as a fiddle." Aunt Gerri held out her arms to him. "Oh! I'm so happy to see you!"

"I'm glad to see you, too, Aunt Gerri." Dylan hugged her and kissed her on the cheek.

"Okay...so let's go inside." Aunt Gerri turned to head back into the house. "You'll have to shut the door real hard—it's been sticking lately."

Dylan ran his hand up the edge of the door. "I'll fix it for you before I leave."

"Oh! Would you?" Aunt Gerri beamed. "That would be such a big help. I was finally going to break down and call someone about it tomorrow. You'll be saving me the trouble. Do you want coffee?"

"No, thanks. I'm good." Dylan stopped to straighten a picture of Uncle Bill hanging in the foyer. After his mom died, this became his permanent home. Uncle Bill and Aunt Gerri took him and raised him. This house, with its creaky wide-planked wooden floors and thick crown molding, was his home. It was the one place that never really changed. The one thing he could always count on, especially when something significant happened in his life.

"Let's go to the sitting room, then. I want to show you my brand-new organ." Aunt Gerri headed into the large room to the left of the foyer.

"It's a Lowrey Holiday Classic..." Aunt Gerri stood proudly by her organ. "I just traded my old one in. This is my seventh organ and this'll probably be the last one I buy..."

Dylan sat down in his grandmother's rocking chair. "It's nice. I like it."

"I'll be sure to play it for you before you go." Aunt Gerri settled herself in another rocking chair. "So..." Her sharp blue eyes were curious. "What's the news?"

"Can't I visit you without being accused of having an ulterior motive?"

"Oh, I think I know you pretty well," Aunt Gerri said. "There's gotta be something real important going on to bring you all the way out here on a business day."

"You've always had my number ever since I was a kid." Dylan fiddled with the loose rocking-chair arm before he looked back at his aunt. "And you're right. There is something I need to tell you."

"Well, go on and tell me what it is so we can talk it out."

"I found out a couple of weeks ago that I have...a daughter." Dylan watched his aunt's face to gauge her reaction. "Her name is Hope. She's ten."

"Did you just say you've got a daughter?" Aunt Gerri stopped rocking. "Who's the mother?"

For the next half hour, Dylan talked and his aunt listened. He told his aunt about the first time he'd ever seen Hope at the barn and he recounted his recent conversation with Mackenzie. Like a confession, he didn't leave anything out. Not even the fact that he hadn't been sober the night Hope had been conceived or the fact that he had never dated Mackenzie. And when he was done, he felt as if a weight had been lifted. Now that Aunt Gerri knew about Hope, it was real. No matter what happened, no matter how tough it got, there was no going back.

When he had said his piece, Aunt Gerri thought a bit before she spoke. She rocked back and forth, mulling things over.

"Now that I think about it, I remember Mackenzie. She was a heavyset girl, wasn't she? But she had beautiful blue eyes."

Dylan nodded. "She still does."

*Violet eyes.*

"She was such a sweet little girl," his aunt said. "But so serious."

"She still is."

"Well…what does she want from you, Dylan? What does she expect?"

"She wants me to spend time with Hope. That's all. She doesn't want money…"

"Not even for the medical bills? Good gracious, cancer treatment can't be cheap." Aunt Gerri had always held the purse strings for the farm.

"I know," Dylan responded to his aunt's skeptical expression. "I thought it was strange, too. But she was adamant about the money. More than that, she doesn't want me to be a parent to Hope, either."

Aunt Gerri frowned. "But is that what *you* want? You're the child's father."

"Honestly, Aunt Gerri? I have no idea what I want."

"Well…I suppose that's where you need to start then, don't you? If you don't know what you want, how in the world can you figure out what you're going to do?"

Hope had picked Pegasus as their first father-and-daughter day. It seemed like a better idea than a restaurant, and he wanted Hope to feel comfortable, so he had agreed. Now that he was here, he started to doubt the soundness of that decision. Perhaps they should have met in private, at his house, *before* they went public. Dylan parked his car next to Mackenzie's Chevy and shut off the engine. Instead of getting out, he stayed in the car. He'd never felt capable of having a panic attack until today. His heart was racing, his mouth was dry and beads of sweat were trickling down the side of his face. He was a mess. The thought of spending the day with Hope made him feel panicked. He had absolutely no idea what to say to a ten-year-old girl; ten-year-old girls hadn't exactly been his target demographic.

"Quit being a coward," Dylan said to himself. "And get out of the stupid car."

After convincing himself to leave the car, Dylan headed to the office. Lucky for him, Aggie was the only one there.

She greeted him with a broad smile and a loud, booming voice. "I heard you were comin' out to lend us a hand today!"

Aggie stomped over to him in her crusty, knee-high black rubber boots and pumped his hand a couple of times. "Come on over here and take a load off. I've got your papers all ready to be filled out. Nothing fancy—but the long and short of it is, you're agreein' that if one of our horses kicks you in the privates or eats your pinkie for a snack, you're on your own. We volunteer at our own risk around here…so if you can live with that, I'll be more than happy to put you to work."

"I can live with it." Dylan sat down at the cluttered picnic table in the middle of the room and resisted the urge to start straightening it up. Instead, he forced himself to focus on reviewing the papers.

"I'll make you a badge so you'll feel official. We don't have riders today—just barn work. But anyone who wants to ride after the chores are done can saddle up."

Aggie handed Dylan a badge and Dylan handed her the filled-out forms. Dylan stood up and Aggie looked down at his pristine boots.

"If you're gonna hang with us, you're gonna have'ta get you some good old-fashioned muckers. Those fancy boots aren't gonna survive a fresh steamin' pile of manure, I guarantee *that*." When Aggie laughed, one eye stayed open and the other one shut completely. "I'm done with ya, so head to the barn. There's always plenty to be done and not enough hands to do it."

Dylan walked out of the office, around the corner, and bumped right into Mackenzie.

Their bodies hit together so hard that Mackenzie had the breath temporarily knocked out of her.

Concerned, Dylan held on to her arms to steady her. "Are you okay?"

"I wasn't expecting anyone to come around that corner," Mackenzie said, slightly annoyed. "But I'm okay now. You can let go."

Dylan released her arms quickly, as if he was pulling his hands away from hot coals. "Sorry. I did it again."

Dylan stared hard at Mackenzie. Something had just happened between them. When their bodies came together, they were a perfect fit. She was curvy and voluptuous and petite; not what he would normally gravitate toward. But he liked the way her body had felt against his. He had enjoyed the feeling of having Mackenzie in his arms. She felt like...home.

Mackenzie tugged on the front of her oversize, long-sleeve T-shirt. "I'm glad you came."

"I said I would," Dylan said defensively.

"I know." Mackenzie had worry etched into her forehead. "I know you did...but I was..."

"Worried that I wouldn't show?"

"Yes...I'm sorry. But, yes. Hope could hardly sleep last night. She's so excited to meet you." Mackenzie was speaking in a low, private voice. "But I think she's more scared than anything."

"Scared? Why is she scared of me?"

"She's not scared *of you.* I think that she's scared that you won't like her." Mackenzie pushed some wayward strands of hair away from her face.

"Well, then, that makes two of us, because I've been really worried that she won't like me, too." Dylan looked down at his outfit. "I changed my clothes three times before I finally put this together."

Mackenzie's eyebrows rose. Dylan was wearing a pressed Ralph Lauren button-down dress shirt, new dark-wash jeans and his spotless boots.

"I did mention that you were going to be doing barn work…didn't I?" Mackenzie asked.

"You mentioned it. I just wanted to look nice for Hope." Dylan frowned down at his outfit. "I look ridiculous, don't I?"

"No. You don't look ridiculous, Dylan. You just look… kind of dressy for the barn. That's all," Mackenzie tried to reassure him. "But stop worrying. Trust me. Hope doesn't care what you're wearing. So…are you ready?"

"Nope." Dylan's stomach started to feel a little queasy.

"What happened to the fearless Dylan Axel I used to know?" Mackenzie tried to tease his nerves away.

"He was too young to know better."

"Come on, Dylan." Mackenzie offered him her hand. "The best way to get something done is to start…"

Dylan took her hand, soft and warm, and let her gently tug him in the right direction. Their hands naturally slipped apart as they walked side by side through the barn's dusty center aisle. As they walked along, Mackenzie greeted the ragtag bunch of secondhand horses and the handful of volunteers working that day. With thirty geriatric horses to care for, Dylan understood why Aggie was so eager to sign him up. Organizations that relied entirely on donations, grants and volunteers were in a constant state of borderline panic and flux. Pegasus was no different.

"This way." Mackenzie tucked her fingers into the front

pocket of her jeans. "Hope's out back washing feed buckets."

Dylan could hear the water running from the hose and he stopped walking. "Wait."

"What's wrong?"

Dylan backed up a step. "Maybe this isn't the best place for this to happen."

"Oh, no, no, no, no, *no*. You're not backing out." Mackenzie's demeanor changed. She walked over to him and grabbed his hand. "This is happening *right now*."

Mackenzie pulled Dylan forward a couple of steps, into an open area with concrete slabs set up for washing the horses.

"Hey, kiddo!" Mackenzie slapped a bright smile on her face. "Look who I found…"

Under her breath, and only for Dylan's ears, Mackenzie said, "You're up."

Hope looked up from her task of washing out a large group of blue feed buckets. She looked at him directly and what he saw in her eyes was something he hadn't experienced with anyone other than his aunt Gerri: total acceptance. Hope's pretty face lit up with excitement as she smiled nervously at him. She dropped the hose and wiped her hands off on her jeans while she headed over to where they were standing. Hope wrapped her arm around her mom's waist for security. She looked up at Mackenzie, Mackenzie looked at Dylan, and Dylan looked at Hope.

"A*wwww*kward." Hope was the first to break the uncomfortable silence.

Dylan liked how Hope broke the ice. "You're right. It is."

Mackenzie ran her hand over the top of Hope's head. "Sometimes this one doesn't have a filter."

"That's okay." Dylan was immediately hooked by

Hope's shy, brief smile. "I have that same problem some-times."

"Do you know who I am?" Hope asked him.

"Hope…" Mackenzie started to correct her.

"No. That's okay," Dylan said to Mackenzie before he looked down at Hope. "Yes. I do know who you are. You're my Hope."

## Chapter Six

"Here…" Hope slipped a blue-and-yellow rubber-band bracelet off her wrist and handed it to him. "I made this for you."

"Hey…thanks." Dylan slipped it over his hand onto his wrist. He held it out for Hope to see. "Does it look good on me?"

Hope nodded. "It's a friendship bracelet."

It took the child of the group to ease the tension, but it took the mom in the group to get things moving along.

"Come on…" Mackenzie squeezed Hope's shoulder. "Let's get back to work. Aggie would have a fit if she saw us all standing around getting nothing done."

The three of them put their nervous energy into finishing Hope's chore together. And it turned out that having a common goal to accomplish eased the tension between them. Of course, it wasn't perfect and there were some odd lulls in conversation. And Dylan caught Hope in the act of studying him when she thought it was safe. Dylan understood her fascination, because he had to resist the urge to stare at his daughter. Mackenzie, on the other hand, made no bones about blatantly watching the two of them interact. But by the time all of the feed buckets were washed and drying in the sun, the tension between them had slowly given way to a more relaxed, fun vibe.

"What next?" Dylan unbuttoned his cuffs and rolled up his sleeves. His shirt was soaked, his boots were already caked with mud, and it made him feel less out of place than when he had arrived.

"Now we have to put all the feed buckets back into the stalls." Hope grabbed some buckets. "Carry as many as you can so we can get done quicker. Then, I get to ride Gypsy."

"Her favorite horse," Mackenzie explained.

Dylan grabbed as many buckets as his fingers could hold. "Lead the way, boss."

His words made Hope laugh, spontaneously and loudly. She smiled at him again, this time without the nervousness. Hope's smile, Dylan decided, was a million-dollar smile. It was addictive. He wanted to see it again and again.

"While you guys do this, I'm going to help Aggie in the office," Mackenzie said. She looked at Hope specifically. "Is that okay?"

When Hope gave a small nod to her mom, Dylan felt as if he had managed to accomplish something pretty major: Hope felt comfortable enough with him to spend time alone. One by one, Hope introduced Dylan formally to the horses and it was obvious that Hope had a special connection with each and every one of them. The horses, some of whom pinned their ears back and gnashed their teeth at him, all came to Hope for some love and attention. It made him feel proud that, at such a young age, she had a special way with these horses. They weren't pretty. They weren't young. But she loved them just the same. In that, she took directly after kindhearted Mackenzie.

"This is Cinnamon." Hope rubbed her hand lovingly over the mare's face. "She's a sweet girl. Aren't you, Cinnamon? When you work with her, make sure you only approach her from her left side, because she's missing her right eye. See?"

Dylan nodded. There was a deep indent where the mare's eye should have been.

"If you walk up to her on her right side, she might get spooked and accidentally knock you over. But she wouldn't mean to hurt you."

After putting the feed bucket in her stall, Hope kissed Cinnamon affectionately on the nose.

"I've saved the best for last," Hope said excitedly. "This…is *Gypsy*."

The word *Gypsy* was said with flair, as if Hope were introducing the most amazing horse in the history of the equine. Dylan read the large plaque on Gypsy's stall: Warning! This horse will bite! Dylan then took a step back from the gate. Hope wrapped her arms around the mare's neck and hugged.

"What's with the sign?" Dylan asked.

"Oh," Hope said nonchalantly. "She's just looking for food, is all. That's why Aggie won't let us carry treats in our pockets. And we can only give them treats in their buckets, never by hand.

"Isn't she great?" Hope rubbed the space between Gypsy's sad brown eyes.

Gypsy was a spindly-legged barrel-bellied mare with giant, fuzzy donkey ears, a dull brown coat and an unusually long, bony face. Even in the best of times, Dylan knew that Gypsy had *never* been a prize.

Wanting to be diplomatic on his first day hanging out

with his daughter, Dylan said the only *noncommittal* thing he could say, "If you like her then I like her."

"I knew you'd like her, too." Hope nodded happily.

In between stuffing envelopes for the upcoming fundraiser, Mackenzie periodically checked on Hope and Dylan by poking her head around the corner. She didn't feel good about spying, but she *had to* check on Hope. And she was glad she did. If she hadn't spied on them, she would have missed a hallmark moment: the expression on her daughter's face when she introduced Dylan to Gypsy. Hope was beaming at him. She knew all of her daughter's many expressions by heart. That one? It was only reserved for those that Hope *really* liked. For Mackenzie, bearing witness to this moment confirmed for her that bringing Dylan into Hope's life was the right thing to do. It didn't nullify her fears for what a future with Dylan in it would mean for *her*, but for Hope? Her trepidation was erased just like words being wiped away on a whiteboard.

"Done!" Hope attached Gypsy's clean feed bucket to the hook in the stall and then exited the stall.

"Nice work." Dylan held up his hand.

Hope high-fived him. "Do you want to help me get Gypsy's tack?"

"Of course I do. I cleared my entire Sunday just for you."

"You did?"

Dylan nodded. He'd managed to win another smile from Hope. He was on a winning streak and felt like hugging her. But he didn't.

"That's cool," Hope said.

Hope grabbed the bridle, girth and saddle pad, while Dylan hoisted the heavy Western saddle onto his hip. With two of them working, they made quick work of grooming Gypsy before tacking her up. By the end of it, Dylan felt proud of the fact that he'd managed to get the job done without being on the losing end of Gypsy's teeth.

"You can ride, too, you know," his daughter said as she walked Gypsy down the breezeway.

"That's okay…I'd rather watch you," he said. He hadn't been on a horse since high school.

Mackenzie heard her daughter's voice in the breezeway and she met them at the barn entrance. There was a moment when she had a front-row seat to Hope and Dylan walking together, side by side, as if they had known each other all their lives. They had the same swing in their walk, these two. The same way of holding their shoulders, the same easygoing, couldn't-possibly-ignore-it kind of smile.

"Hey, Mom!" Hope greeted Mackenzie enthusiastically. "I was just telling Dylan all about the riding school I want to open up after college."

"I didn't even know they made ten-year-olds like this." Dylan smiled at them.

"Sometimes I don't believe that she's ten." Mackenzie handed Hope a bottle of water. "Hydration, sunscreen and helmet, please."

Mackenzie raised her eyebrows at Dylan over Hope's head. Dylan smiled at her and gave her the "okay" symbol.

"Sunscreen." Mackenzie exchanged the water bottle for the sunscreen bottle.

Hope put sunscreen on her arms and her face. She handed the sunscreen bottle back to Mackenzie along with Gypsy's reins.

"I'll be right back." Hope jogged over to the tack room to grab a helmet.

"How's it going?" Mackenzie asked quietly.

"Good," Dylan said. "Really good…"

"I was hoping that the two of you would…you know… figure each other out if I gave you some space."

"I think we did okay," Dylan said. "She's an incredible kid, Mackenzie. I mean…my God. So smart."

"Straight As," Mackenzie said with pride. "Even when she was at her worst with the chemo."

"I like her." Dylan's thoughts became words.

Mackenzie wasn't a crier. But when Dylan quietly said that he liked Hope, she felt like weeping with relief.

"Well…" Mackenzie turned her head away from him until she could put a halt to the waterworks. "I can tell that she's already crazy about you."

"Yeah? Do you think so?" Dylan was temporarily distracted by how the sunlight was reflecting on Mackenzie's face. It looked dewy and flushed and pretty. Her lips, lips that he'd never really noticed before, were naturally pink and plump. Kissable lips.

"I do." Mackenzie nodded. "I do."

Mackenzie liked how disheveled Dylan looked now. Gone was the catalog model posed in a barn. Part of his shirt was untucked, his jeans were dirty and the once-pristine boots were caked with mud and manure. He was sweaty and grimy and she liked him like that.

Irritated with her own musings about Dylan's masculine appeal, she decided to razz him the way she did when they were kids. "I bet your manicurist is going to have a heck of a time cleaning your nails."

Dylan checked his nails. "Yeah…you're probably right."

"I was just *kidding*! Don't tell me you really *do* have a manicurist, Dylan!"

"In my line of business, being well groomed is a matter of survival."

"Oh, dear Lord…" Mackenzie rolled her eyes. "I can't believe I've actually seen the day when Dylan Axel willingly submitted to a manicure. What happened to the guy who used to love to have grease up to his elbows?"

"Hey…there's nothing wrong with a guy taking care of himself. In fact…*ow*!" Dylan swung his head around quick. "She *bit* me!"

"What?"

Dylan glared at the mare accusingly. "You *bit* me!"

"Where'd she get you?" Mackenzie looked him over. "I don't see any teeth marks."

"That's because she didn't *bite* me on the arm." Dylan scowled at the mare. "Did you, you glue factory reject?"

Hope interrupted their conversation when she returned with a helmet. "What happened?"

"Nothing worth talking about. Here, kiddo." Mackenzie handed Hope the reins. "Why don't you get started and we'll be right behind you, okay."

"Okay. Come on, Gyps!" Hope led Gypsy to the riding arena.

When Hope was out of earshot, Mackenzie said, "She bit you on the butt, didn't she?"

"Let's put it this way…" Dylan said sourly. "It's going to be a long painful drive back to the city."

"Wait here." Mackenzie tried very hard to stifle her smile but failed. "I'll be right back"

Mackenzie returned with Aggie in tow.

"All right." Aggie held a first-aid kit in her hand. "Where'd she getcha? I swear that mare gets meaner every year…"

Mackenzie blurted out, "She bit him in the butt."

"Once a tattletale…" Dylan muttered.

"I'm not a bit surprised," Aggie said. "That's one of her favorite spots… She's gotten me on the fleshy part a couple of times. Do you want me to take a look? See if she broke the skin?"

"No, thank you!" Dylan stepped back.

"Oh, come on, Dylan…" Mackenzie teased him. "Don't be such a baby. Let Aggie take a look."

"Thank *you*," Dylan said to Aggie, then to Mackenzie, "But *no*."

"Suit yourself. But I suggest you grow eyeballs in the back of your head so you can see for yourself if she broke the skin." Aggie handed him the first-aid kit and headed back to the office. "And remember…you volunteered at your own risk."

"Which way to the bathroom?" Dylan asked Mackenzie.

"This way." Mackenzie smirked.

"I suppose you think this is funny…?"

"Not at all."

*"Liar!"* Dylan smiled at her. "What happened to the girl who used to have a little integrity, huh?"

"Here's the bathroom." Mackenzie pointed. "Light switch on the left."

Dylan went into the bathroom and examined his backside by turning his back to the mirror and straining his neck to look over his shoulder.

"Damn if she didn't break the skin." Dylan ripped open a packet containing an alcohol wipe. He dabbed the wound and then closed his eyes when the alcohol hit it. "And that smarts…"

"How's it going in there?" Mackenzie called through the door.

"She got me good." Dylan tossed the used wipe into the trash.

"Make sure you put some ointment on it and a Band-Aid."

"I'm not a contortionist, Mackenzie." Dylan pulled up his underwear carefully.

After a pause, Mackenzie asked, "Do you want me to do it?"

"It's fine."

"If you don't put something on it, won't it hurt worse when you drive home?"

"I'll manage." Dylan pulled up his jeans.

Mackenzie knocked on the door. "Why don't you let me help you?"

Not waiting for his response, Mackenzie turned the doorknob. "I'm coming in."

Dylan tried to lock the door but the lock failed.

"That lock's been broken for about a year now." Mackenzie leaned her hand against the doorjamb. "Will you stop pretending to be a prude and let me help you?"

"Really? You just open the door and waltz right in? What if I had been in the *middle* of something?"

"I could see your boots near the sink, okay? Now, quit whining and turn around."

"Mackenzie…" Dylan said. "The bite is on my *ass*."

"So? Do you think that I haven't seen your butt before? Give me a break! You and my brother and all of your stupid friends mooned everyone in the neighborhood! Remember?"

"Oh, yeah…I forgot about that."

"What did you idiots used to call yourselves again?"

"The Moonshine Gang."

"I'm sorry…" Mackenzie cupped her ear. "I didn't quite catch that?"

"The Moonshine Gang," Dylan said loudly.

"Thank you. I rest my case. Now, turn around, drop trou, then hand me the ointment. Please."

Grudgingly, Dylan turned around and dropped his jeans just enough to expose the wound.

"She got you, all right." Mackenzie squeezed some ointment onto the wound. "Hand me one of the big, square Band-Aids, will you?"

Mackenzie ripped open the package with her teeth.

"What's going on back there?" Dylan asked impatiently.

"I'm baking a cake…what do you think's going on?" Mackenzie pulled the Band-Aid out of the packet and tossed the empty wrapper into the trash.

"Voilà!" Mackenzie quickly applied the Band-Aid. "Done!"

Mackenzie left the bathroom while Dylan straightened his clothes.

"You're welcome," Mackenzie said when he joined her.

"*You* should be apologizing to *me* for barging into the bathroom like that," Dylan countered with feigned indignation.

"*You* should be apologizing for having a manicurist!" Mackenzie retorted.

Dylan stuck out his hand. "Call it even?"

"Fine. Even." Mackenzie shook Dylan's hand. "Come on…let's go watch Hope ride."

They walked out to the riding arena and both of them leaned up against the fence. Dylan watched Hope canter Gypsy. "She's got a great seat for riding."

"She definitely doesn't get that from me. I've always been a little afraid of horses."

"No. *That* she gets from me."

Mackenzie glanced at Dylan. They had known each other in another lifetime, when they were just kids. But there was something comfortable in their silences when it was just the two of them. That *something* was familiar, unrehearsed, effortless and impossible to fake. There was a shared history; they came from the same neighborhood. There was a common thread of values that transcended the years they had spent apart.

When Dylan spoke, it was in a lowered voice and for her ears only. "I know you told me that Hope has leukemia. But it doesn't seem possible. Just look at her. She's… perfect. She acts like a typical kid."

"She's been in remission for two years, so she's gained weight. And even though it's different and that bothers her, her hair finally grew back. But we aren't out of the woods yet. When she was diagnosed, she was put in the high-risk category, which means she has a greater risk of the cancer coming back."

"You know, when you told me about Hope, about her diagnosis, I've really tried to educate myself about her type of leukemia."

"ALL…"

"Right…" Dylan nodded. "But I still don't know what any of it means for Hope."

"What do you mean?"

Dylan turned his body toward her. "Is she going to be okay or not?"

Mackenzie looked at her daughter, so happy to be riding Gypsy again. "I don't know, Dylan. There's no guarantee. Her prognosis is good, but until we hit the three-year mark without a relapse, *I'm* not going to feel like we're out of the woods yet. She takes daily doses of medication, she goes in for regular testing and she still takes chemo. And let me tell you, when she does have chemo, she's not the same kid. She can't get out bed, she's sick to her stomach, I can hardly get her to eat." Mackenzie watched her daughter. "That's why she pushes herself so hard in between…"

"Because she knows what she's in for…"

"Exactly." Mackenzie smiled and waved at Hope, who cantered in a circle directly in front of them.

"She never mentioned it to me." Dylan rested his foot on the bottom of the fence. "I sort of thought she would."

"She doesn't like to talk about it much anymore, and I

try to respect that. All she wants is to be a normal kid. Who can blame her? No kid should have to go through this…"

Dylan wasn't certain what had changed inside him. But something had. A switch had been flipped, an indelible mark had been made, and there wasn't any going back. When he had awakened this morning, he hadn't been a father…and perhaps he really wasn't still. But he *wanted* to be. He saw it now just as plainly as if it had been written across the cloudless blue sky…he had a chance to do better for Hope. He had a choice…he could reject the legacy left to him by his biological father and embrace the lessons he had learned from Uncle Bill. And it took Hope, sweet, honest, tenderhearted Hope, to make him see the light. Hope slowed Gypsy to a jog and then an animated walk. Gypsy's neck was drenched with sweat, her mouth dripping foam from engaging with the bit.

Cheeks flushed red, eyes bright with joy, Hope patted Gypsy enthusiastically on the neck. "Good girl, Gypsy! I'm going to take her for a walk to cool her down before I rinse her off." Hope dropped her feet out of the stirrups and let them dangle loose.

"I'll grab the gate for you," Mackenzie said.

Hope guided Gypsy through the arena gate and headed to an open field; Mackenzie and Dylan walked slowly back toward the barn.

"Have you told Jordan yet that I'm Hope's father?" Dylan asked in a low, private voice.

"No." She had led her family to believe that her college boyfriend was Hope's father. Only her father and brother knew the truth. It was hard to come clean on a lie, especially one as big as this one.

"I haven't told Ian yet, either." Dylan slipped his sunglasses back on. "I'll call him and see if we can get together with them tonight. We may as well tell them together."

## Chapter Seven

Mackenzie and Dylan took the elevator up to Ian Sterling's penthouse. Dylan, Mackenzie noted, was impeccably dressed in pressed khaki slacks, a custom-tailored navy blazer and spotless shoes that had to have cost more than one month's rent. She, on the other hand, still had on her baking clothes: an oversize Nothin' But Cupcakes polo, new black Converse and an old pair of baggy chinos that were permanently stained with food dye.

Mackenzie took a small step away from Dylan. Whenever she was near him, she felt like a dumpy bag lady. She caught her reflection in the highly polished brass elevator fittings. Had she been having an odd Alfalfa moment this whole entire time? She quickly tried to smooth the out-of-control curls.

Mackenzie glanced over at Dylan, who was standing stiffly next to her. He looked as nervous as she felt. "So... how's your backside?"

Her attempt to get him to loosen up a little worked. He cracked a smile. "Sore. Thank you for asking."

"Well…you're not the first victim."

"And I won't be the last…" The elevator came to a slow stop, the light dinged. "This is us."

In front of the condo's ornate door, Mackenzie started to feel queasy from nerves. Telling your family that you've been lying to them for ten years didn't exactly seem like a fun time. When Dylan opened the unlocked door, she wished she were anyplace other than where she was.

"Anybody home?" Dylan announced their arrival.

"Dylan! Mackenzie!" Barefoot, dressed in faded low-slung boy jeans and a simple white tee, Jordan appeared at the top of the stairwell leading up to the main floor.

"Come on up! I apologize in advance for the renovation mess…"

At the top of the stairs, Jordan hugged Mackenzie first, and then Dylan.

"Jordan…this view…"

"I know, right? Crazy good. Once it's remodeled, it's going to be heaven on earth…"

"She's taking advantage of the fact that I can't see the invoices," Jordan's fiancé, Ian, commented as he walked into the room.

Mackenzie had seen pictures of Ian Sterling, world-renowned photographer and ex-model, but to see him in person was an entirely different experience. He was tall and built, high cheekbones, strong jawline. Sculpted lips. He was a perfect physical match for tall, athletic, naturally beautiful Jordan.

Jordan went immediately to Ian's side and linked arms with him. "Knock that off, *GQ*… Mackenzie doesn't know you're kidding. I'm just warning you guys. He's been cracking a lot of blind jokes lately…" Jordan confided to

Mackenzie as she nonchalantly guided Ian over to where Dylan and Mackenzie were standing.

"And Jordan is determined to suck all the fun out of this little adventure…" Ian said about his blindness.

Even though it was dusk, Ian wore dark sunglasses. Diagnosed with a rare form of macular degeneration called Stargardt disease, Ian was legally blind.

Jordan had a glow about her that Mackenzie envied. No man had ever made her all girlie and dewy and *flushed*.

Jordan introduced Mackenzie and Ian. They shook hands, and then Ian and Dylan gave each other a hug.

"Let's talk in the study…it's the only room Jordan hasn't torn apart…"

"Yet…" Jordan wrapped her arms around Ian's body and squeezed him tightly. "You know you love me."

Ian dropped a kiss on the top of Jordan's head. "Yes, I do…"

They all grabbed drinks and then headed to the study. There were two love seats on either side of the coffee table. Jordan curled up next to Ian on one love seat, which left the other one for Mackenzie and Dylan. Dylan waited for her to be seated before he joined her. No matter how she tried, she couldn't avoid touching Dylan's body. They were shoulder to shoulder and leg to leg on the tiny love seat.

"Okay…" Jordan got the conversation started. "I'm about to keel over with curiosity. What are the two of you doing here…*together*?"

Mackenzie and Dylan exchanged looks.

"Do you want to tell them?" Dylan asked her. "Or should I?"

"I'll do it. I'm the one who got us into this mess…"

"Well…I hardly think that's the case. It took both of us to—"

Exasperated, Jordan interrupted. "For the love of God

and all that is holy in the world…will you *please* tell us what's going on?"

Ian touched Jordan's leg to get her attention. "What?"

"Let them talk," Ian said gently.

Jordan frowned at Ian but gave Mackenzie and Dylan the floor.

"I have to set the record straight about something." Mackenzie wiped more sweat from her palms onto her pant legs. "Dylan is Hope's father."

Mackenzie's abrupt confession was followed by silence. Like a pretty kaleidoscope, Jordan's facial expression changed from confusion to shock to disbelief.

"I'm sorry…what did you just say?" Jordan leaned forward a bit.

"Hope is Dylan's child," Mackenzie repeated. It actually felt good to get this out in the open. She had never liked lying to her family. She had wanted to keep it from her father and Jett so they wouldn't tell Dylan, but the lie had metastasized to the rest of the family.

Jordan stared at the two of them, speechless in her contemplation, and Ian hadn't said a word. He was just listening, taking it all in.

"I'm Hope's father." That was the first time he had uttered those words aloud to anyone other than himself. "Hope is my daughter."

Jordan sat back. "Wait a minute…you mean…*Hope* Hope? As in, *your* daughter, Hope?"

Mackenzie nodded silently.

"But…I thought Hope's father was your boyfriend from college…the one with all the Star Wars toys…"

"Star Trek," Mackenzie corrected. "He was a Trekkie…"

Jordan rolled her eyes. "Whatever…same difference."

"Not to a Trekkie," Ian said. "They're completely different."

Jordan twisted around to look at Ian. "Really? Now you decide to chime in?"

"He's right," Dylan agreed. "Two completely different things."

"Can we get back to the important part of this conversation, please?" Jordan looked at everyone questioningly. "I mean…how do the two of you even *know* each other?"

The conversation that followed took longer than Mackenzie had originally anticipated. She was hoping for a more "drive-by" kind of deal that didn't require much emotional energy. That didn't happen. While Ian remained quiet for the entire conversation, he appeared to be listening intently to every word. Jordan, on the other hand, decided to earn her junior Perry Mason badge.

"Look…" Mackenzie finally said, exasperated. "I wasn't signing up for the Spanish Inquisition here, okay? I was young and I thought I was doing the right thing for all of us. Would I do it this way again?" Mackenzie caught Dylan's eye and held it. "No. I wouldn't." Mackenzie broke the gaze. To her cousin, she said, "But I can't go back. All I can do is say that I'm sorry for lying to you. I wasn't trying to hurt anyone. I was just trying to do the best I could for Hope. That's what I'm still trying to do…"

"Oh…hey…" Jordan crossed the short distance to Mackenzie's seat and wrapped her arms around her cousin's shoulders. "I didn't mean to upset you. I'm just surprised, that's all. I love you, Mackenzie. And I love Hope…no matter what. Okay?"

Jordan knelt down beside Mackenzie. "Hey…let me give you the five-cent tour of this place. I want to show you all the finishes I've picked…hand-scraped wide-plank hardwood…new custom cabinets throughout…"

"Hey—I *heard* that," Ian told his fiancée. "I still have excellent hearing."

Jordan laughed and returned to Ian's side. She leaned down, took his gorgeous face into her hands and kissed him on the lips. "I love you, my handsome man…"

"I love you more." Ian squeezed her hand, kissed it affectionately before letting it go.

Dylan watched Mackenzie and Jordan leave the room. He waited several seconds to make certain they were out of earshot before he said to Ian, "You haven't had much to say."

"Not much to say, I don't think." Ian pulled his wallet out of his pocket. He pulled a card out of the wallet, brought the card close to the side of his face so he could use his still-intact peripheral vision to read the name, then he held it out to Dylan. "Here. You might need this."

*Ben Levine, Attorney-at-Law.*

After looking at it, Dylan slipped the card into his wallet.

"You have a child." Ian twisted the cap off his bottle of water. "How do you feel about that?"

"Terrified." Dylan could be honest with Ian.

"You need to know your rights. We have the photography business to think of…we're launching the modeling agency in a couple of months…"

"I know. Mackenzie doesn't want child support, but…"

"People change their minds all the time. Call Ben."

"I will." Dylan nodded pensively. "You know…I spent the whole morning with her today. Hope. She's a great kid. Looks just like Aunt Gerri."

"Is that right?"

"Yeah…" Dylan smiled when an image of Hope's sweet, expectant face popped into his head. "Do you want to meet her?"

"Of course I do. She's your daughter." Ian finished off his water. "I'm not saying you shouldn't get involved...I'm just saying that you should cover your bases. That's all."

"Expect the best..." Dylan said.

Ian finished their motto. "But prepare for the worst."

After their visit with Jordan and Ian, Mackenzie and Dylan rode the elevator down to the ground floor together. Through the lobby of the building and out onto the city sidewalk, they paused for a moment just outside the front door. Noticing a large group of tourists heading their way, Dylan put his hand on the small of her back and guided her to the left. Then he put his body between hers and the group so she wouldn't get bumped.

Once the boisterous group passed them by, Mackenzie said, "You didn't have to leave when I did. You could have stayed."

Dylan had his hands in his front pockets, his blazer thrown over his arm. "It was time for me to head out, too. Did you walk here from the bakery?"

Mackenzie nodded.

"I'll walk you back," he said. Even though downtown San Diego was a pretty safe place, even at dusk, he didn't like the idea of her walking back to the bakery alone.

"It's not that far..." She looked over her shoulder toward the direction of her business.

But once she saw that Dylan was going to insist on seeing her safely back to Nothin' But Cupcakes, Mackenzie stopped protesting and started walking. At a crosswalk, waiting for the light to turn, she asked, "What does your girlfriend think of all this?"

The light turned and Dylan stepped into the crosswalk at her side. "Actually, Jenna and I had an amicable parting of the ways..."

"Not because of Hope?" She stepped up onto the curb.

"No. Not because of Hope." He reassured her. "She decided to finally make the move to LA, and I support her decision. It's what's best for her career. The breakup was inevitable."

"Well…I'm still sorry. She seemed really—" she searched her brain for a positive comment that she could say truthfully "—energetic."

Dylan shot her a quizzical look before he laughed. "Yes…you're right. She is very energetic."

They reached her storefront and Mackenzie pulled the keys out of her tote bag. "Well…this is me. Thanks for walking me back."

"Are you heading home or sticking around here?"

She slipped the key into the lock. "I have some work to do before I head home."

Mackenzie opened the door and walked quickly to the alarm keypad. She punched in the code and the beeping sound stopped. The only light in the front of the bakery was from the cases that had been emptied the night before by Molly.

"Thank you again for making sure I got here safely," she said to Dylan, who had followed her in and locked the door behind them. "But I'm sure you've got things to do. I'll be fine here by myself."

Sometimes she liked to come to the bakery after hours just to have some time alone—Ray and Charlie were always happy to watch Hope for her. She liked the bakery when it was quiet and dark the way it was now. She could be by herself with her thoughts while she baked. It was therapeutic, especially when she had something worrisome on her mind.

He knew she was politely trying to send him on his way, but he wasn't ready to leave just yet. He was enjoying her company. He felt relaxed around her; she made him laugh in a way that most women didn't.

"My schedule's pretty clear, actually. How about a quick tour?"

He heard her let out her breath and knew she was about to cave. "There's not much to see…and I really do have work that I've got to get done."

"I promise I'll stay out of your way…" He held up one hand as if he was taking an oath.

For the second time that night, Mackenzie gave in to Dylan's persistence. She was wasting time talking to him when she really needed to be working on the cupcakes. Molly had called to tell her that they were about to run out of one of their bestsellers, red velvet with cream cheese frosting. It was her mother's recipe, so she guarded it. She was the only one who made them; she needed to make several large batches and freeze some of them for later.

"I could help you," Dylan offered.

Mackenzie slipped into her white baking coat. "You can help me by sitting over there and not moving."

He smiled at her no-nonsense way of bossing him around her kitchen and obediently sat down on a stool out of the way. It was interesting to see Mackenzie in her element. Here, in the kitchen, she was absolutely sure of herself. She gathered the ingredients for the cupcakes first, and then measured each ingredient carefully before adding them, one by one, to an industrial mixer. While the batter mixed, she prepared the baking pans, deftly dropping specially designed Nothin' But Cupcakes cupcake cups into the pans. In the zone now, she didn't even seem to notice that he was sitting nearby.

Dylan had never really cared about watching someone cook before, but watching Mackenzie was different. He was fascinated by how easily she moved from one area of the kitchen to the next; it was like watching a well-choreographed dance.

"What kind of frosting are you going to make?" he asked.

Mackenzie glanced up at him, with a somewhat surprised expression in her pretty eyes. He had been so quiet, and she had been so focused, that she forgot for a moment that she wasn't alone.

"Cream cheese." She switched off the mixer and then set to the task of filling the cupcake pans.

Once the cupcakes were baking in the ovens, she made the frosting, which she could store in the refrigerator until morning. Now all she had to do was wait for the cupcakes to cook and cool. With a satisfied sigh, hands on hips, Mackenzie nodded to herself. Then she looked over at Dylan, who hadn't really bothered her at all.

"Do you like cream cheese frosting?"

Dylan had been leaning on one elbow. He sat upright. "Yes. I do."

Mackenzie took a large spoon out of a drawer, scooped up a large helping of freshly made frosting and handed it to him. Dylan ate all the frosting at one time; he closed his eyes happily and then licked the spoon before he handed it back to her.

"Good?" she asked, but she could tell by his smiling lips that he approved.

"Mackenzie…" he said seriously. "You are an artist."

His sincere praise for her baking made her entire body smile. When someone truly enjoyed her baking, it made the struggle to keep her business afloat worth it. Mackenzie felt herself relaxing with Dylan; after all, this wasn't the first time he had loitered in her kitchen. He was always hanging around with Jett when she had baked with her mother.

"Do you want to wait for the cupcakes to finish baking? I'll frost one just for you."

He looked more like the young boy she remembered when he asked, "Just one?"

The month after he first met his daughter sped by for Dylan. And even though he hadn't intended to become a regular fixture at Pegasus, that's exactly what had happened. It started out innocently. It was an opportunity for him to spend time with Hope on the weekends. Then something unexpected happened: the place got to him. The kids, the horses, the other volunteers…the parents… all of them had an impact. He discovered that he was surfing less and mucking out stalls more. He was handy with a hammer and Aggie had him on her radar. On the weekends, he traded his Testoni lace-ups for rubber muckers and his polo button-ups for Pegasus T-shirts. Instead of going out with his friends, he went to bed early on Friday night so he could be up early and fresh for the riders on Saturday morning.

And always, *always*, there was Hope. She was the main event. He found himself missing her during the week and regretting having to say goodbye on Sundays. He didn't mind the status quo for now, but this arrangement wouldn't work in the long term. He wanted to have a say in Hope's future; he wanted to be her *dad*.

"Hey…" Mackenzie appeared at the entrance of the feed room. As usual, she was dressed in oversize clothing, long sleeves, and her hair was haphazardly pulled up into a ponytail. Dylan wished she would fix herself up every once in a while.

"Hey…" Dylan pulled a bale of hay off the tall stack in the corner and dropped it on the ground.

"Where's Hope?"

Dylan used the bottom of his T-shirt to wipe the sweat that was dripping off his face, exposing his stomach. She was human. She looked. And her eyes latched on to the barely visible trail of hair leading from Dylan's belly button directly to his...

Dylan dropped his shirt; when she looked up at him, he was smiling at her. His expression told the story; he'd caught her red-handed.

"She's helping Aggie with Hank—he's got a pretty nasty gash on his fetlock and you know how he feels about anyone messing with his hooves." Dylan hoisted the bale of hay onto his shoulder. "Excuse me."

Mackenzie stepped to the side so Dylan could move through the door. She had watched Dylan closely over the past couple of weekends. She couldn't deny that he had a special way with all the kids, especially Hope. They all loved him. When they could, they trailed after him, and he was happy to let them. He had become the Pegasus Pied Piper. It was...endearing. And Aggie, who was pretty tough to impress, had come to rely on Dylan as part of her small circle of trusted volunteers.

"Do you feel like lending a hand?" Dylan cut the twine holding the bale of hay together.

"Sure."

Loaded down with armfuls of hay, Dylan tackled one side of the barn and Mackenzie tackled the other. When Mackenzie reached Hank's stall, she tossed the hay over the stall fence for the old gelding.

"Hey, Aggie. Time to wrap up, kiddo," Mackenzie said to Hope, who was watching Aggie treat Hank's wound. "You have school tomorrow."

"Okay, Mom...I'll be right there."

Mackenzie waited for Hope at the barn entrance and watched the sun set on the horizon. All day, every day, it seemed as if she was running around like a chicken with her head cut off—monitoring Hope's health, helping Hope with homework, working in the bakery, paying the bills, shopping for groceries, doing the laundry…one chore led into the next, one day bled into the other. She couldn't remember the last time she had actually allowed herself to just stop and enjoy a sunset.

"It's going to be a full moon." Dylan came up beside her.

Not wanting to expend her limited resource of energy on small talk, Mackenzie only nodded. She wanted to enjoy the view just a little bit longer before she had to rally the energy to cook dinner and do a load of laundry. She was having a perfectly lovely time until she felt something crawling on her neck. Startled, she slapped at the side of her neck and tried to spot the offending bug.

Dylan, looking sheepish, held a piece of hay in his fingertips. "You had a piece of hay stuck in your hair."

"Don't *do* that!" Mackenzie punched Dylan hard on the arm. "I thought it was a bug!"

Dylan rubbed his arm. "Man…you really know how to pack a punch…"

"Of course I do… You and Jett and the rest of your idiot friends thought it was hilarious to ambush me with dead bugs all the time! I *had* to learn how to defend myself."

"I never did that to you!"

"Yeah…you did."

"Well, I don't remember doing that, but if you said that I did, then I suppose I'm sorry."

"Your apology, however halfhearted, is accepted."

Dylan glanced over his shoulder; Aggie and Hope were coming out of Hank's stall and his window of opportunity was about to close.

"Mackenzie…" Dylan crossed his arms to give them

something to do. "I was wondering…do you want to come over for dinner Friday night?"

"Um…we can't. Hope's spending the weekend with one of her friends from Relay For Life. I don't normally let her spend an overnight, but this family knows the drill because their daughter has ALL as well, so…"

"I know. Hope told me. That's all she talked about today was her sleepover, which she *never* gets to do. What I meant was…do *you* want to come over Friday night for dinner…with me?"

Mackenzie lifted her brows questioningly. "Why?"

Dylan looked at her as if he couldn't quite figure her out. Perhaps he was used to automatic yeses to all his invitations.

"Because…" he said. "I think it'd be good for us to spend some time together. There are a lot of things we still need to figure out. Don't you agree?"

"I suppose." Up until now, she had been very good at dodging Dylan's attempts to sit down and discuss how they were going to move forward as coparents.

Dylan tucked his hands into his pockets and lifted his shoulders questioningly. "Oh, come on, Mackenzie… what's the worst that could happen? If nothing else, you'll get a free meal out of the deal. And, I really didn't want to brag…"

"Of course not…"

"But I *have* been told that I'm pretty amazing with my grill."

## *Chapter Eight*

Mackenzie stood in front of her closet, staring at the sad collection of old clothing hanging askew on wire hangers. After several attempts at finding something even remotely fashionable to wear to Dylan's house for dinner, Mackenzie groaned dramatically and threw herself face down on her unmade bed. Dylan always looked so put together; she wanted at least to *try*, for her own sake, to look halfway decent for a change. But, in truth, she didn't really want to go at all. What she *really* wanted to do with her first kid-free weekend was to procure a bag of ranch-flavored Doritos and to watch the Food Network in bed. When her cell started to ring, she reached out with her hand and felt around on the nightstand for the phone. Not lifting her head up, she put the phone to her ear.

"Hello?"

"What are you doing?" It was Rayna calling.

"Slowly suffocating myself with my hypoallergenic pillow…"

"I take it the hunt for an outfit isn't going so well?"

Mackenzie rolled onto her back and wrapped herself in her comforter like a burrito. "I think I'm going to call him and tell him I'm too tired…"

"I'm coming over…"

"Is that gangsta rap?" Mackenzie took a time-out from her own crisis and tuned her ear to the loud music blasting through the phone.

"Yes. Charlie had a bad day at work. Max and I are coming over."

Moments later, Rayna and her rotund feline arrived in her bedroom. She peeled the comforter back and found Mackenzie inside. Max jumped up onto her bed with a grunt. He nudged her hand so she would pet him.

"Mackenzie…you can't back out. How long has it been since you've done anything remotely fun?"

Mackenzie tried to remember but couldn't.

"If you have to think about it for *that long*, then it's been *way too* long. And do you know what I think? I think that hidden beneath these rumpled, oversize clothes is a beautiful, curvy woman just dying to come out and play." Rayna tugged on Mackenzie's arm until she was upright. "Now… you go take a shower because you smell really sweaty. Max and I will try to find you something less…boxy to wear."

Needing to clean up anyway, Mackenzie took a quick shower and shrugged into her bathrobe. She wiped the moisture from the bathroom mirror and frowned at her own reflection. She looked tired. Dark circles, a little bit of stress acne on her chin.

*Lovely.*

When Mackenzie returned to her bedroom, her dirty

clothes had been collected and deposited in the hamper. And Max was happily lounging on her freshly made bed.

"What did you do in here?" Mackenzie asked.

"Oh…I just picked up a little so I could see what we're working with," Rayna said offhandedly. "You do know that *square* isn't a flattering shape for a woman's body, right?" Rayna had pulled several tops out of her closet. "Why are all your clothes two sizes too big?"

"I don't have time for shopping, Ray…you know what I *do* have time for?" She sounded defensive. "Payroll. And hospital visits. So, no offense, but having a fashion *moment* just isn't high up on my priority list."

"I know how busy you are." Rayna's hands stilled and she looked over her shoulder at Mackenzie. "But you're still buying clothes for your *old* body. And you may not believe me, but a good pair of jeans and a pretty blouse can change your whole outlook on life."

Mackenzie caught her reflection in the dresser mirror. Yes, she had lost a ton of weight. But when she looked in the mirror, all she saw was *fat*. And, with Hope's illness and always struggling to make ends meet, it was easier just to buy oversize, comfy clothes and avoid reflective surfaces. She couldn't remember the last time she had actually tried something on in a fitting room.

"Now, *this* is pretty!" Rayna spun around and held up a deep purple short-sleeved blouse that Hope had convinced her to buy. "What do you think? It still has the price tag on it."

Mackenzie shook her head. "No. I don't do short sleeves. My arms are too…" She wrinkled her nose distastefully. *"Jiggly."*

Disappointed, Rayna hung the blouse back in the closet. "You're your own worst enemy…you're hot and you don't even know it."

Mackenzie opened her dresser drawer and pulled out her favorite long-sleeved San Diego Padres shirt. "It's ridiculous that I've even been spending *one second* stressing about this...it's *Dylan*. Not a *date*. So I'm not gonna get all gussied up, when I *never* get all gussied up, and make Dylan feel all weirded out because *he* thinks that *I* think that this evening is something more than it is. Which it's not."

"It's a date." Rayna sat down on the bed next to Max. "Friday night. And he's cooking you dinner at his place? It's a date."

Refusing to indulge in Rayna's fantasy, Mackenzie stepped into the bathroom to slip into the Padres shirt and a pair of jeans. Mackenzie sighed. The jeans were tighter around the waist than they used to be. Why did it always have to be such a battle? If she didn't watch every bite, consider every carb or exercise several times a week, the scale would turn against her.

*Whatever.*

"Trust me, Ray...I'm not Dylan's type." Mackenzie grabbed her comb and began the chore of untangling her thick, wavy hair. "And he's not really mine."

"You actually have to *date* to have a type...and besides, you guys have a daughter...you must've been attracted to each other at some point. Right?"

"That was—" Mackenzie stopped combing her hair for a second to think. "I don't know what that was."

"A night of unforgettable passion?" Rayna raised her eyebrows suggestively several times.

Mackenzie scrunched up her face. "Uh-uh. Honestly... it was...really, really *awkward*."

"Oh..." Rayna wilted. "See...judging from pictures, I would've thought Dylan would be good in bed. For a man. He's got that sexy, squinty-eye thing going on."

"I don't know what you're talking about." Mackenzie had never noticed Dylan having a sexy, squinty anything. It was *Dylan*. Annoying, mooning, bug-throwing *Dylan*.

Rayna held up her pinkie and wiggled it. "Is he really… you know? Tiny?"

"What?" Mackenzie looked perplexed at Rayna's bouncing pinkie for a minute before she caught Rayna's meaning. "No…*no*. He's *fine* in that department. It's just that we had way too much to drink…"

"Which never works in a guy's favor…"

"And I didn't want him to touch me anywhere because I was *bulgy* all over…."

Rayna's brows lifted. "Now I'm actually kind of surprised the two of you managed to procreate."

"That's what I've been trying to tell you." Mackenzie twisted her hair up into a bun and secured it with a clip. "I can guarantee you that neither one of us wants a repeat of that night."

Deflated, Rayna said, "So…not a date."

"No. Definitely not a date."

Dylan met her at the door, stylish, freshly showered and shaved. Not a surprise; he even managed to make sweaty and dirty at the barn look good. What *was* a surprise was the table setting. Dylan had obviously put some thought into setting the table for two. There were two lit candles on the table that caught, and held, her attention.

"Now that you're here, I'm going to throw the salmon on the grill. You said you liked salmon, right?"

Mackenzie slipped her tote off her shoulder. "Yes…"

"Make yourself at home and I'll be right back. Unless you want to keep me company…?"

"No." Instead of putting the tote down, Mackenzie clutched it to her body. "I'll wait here."

*I'm on a date.*

Panic. Sheer unadulterated panic. Mackenzie quickly texted Ray: I'm on a DATE!

Ray shot a text back: Told U so! Yippee!

"Yippee? That's the sage advice I get?" Mackenzie turned the phone on Vibrate and tucked it into her pocket. *Now what?*

Should she leave or should she stay...*that* was the ultimate question.

"All right..." Dylan reappeared and headed for the fridge. "I hope you like sweet red wine...?"

Mackenzie nodded. She was still trying to figure out how to back out of this situation gracefully. Could she fake a stomachache? Menstrual cramps? It's not that she didn't want to be on a date with *Dylan* per se...she didn't want to be on a date with *anyone*. Relationships took time and energy and she had very little of both of those resources to spare.

Dylan poured the wine, handed her a glass and then held his glass up for a toast. "To Hope's continued health..."

Mackenzie touched her glass to his. "To Hope's continued health..."

"And to new beginnings," Dylan added.

Mackenzie hesitated before she took a sip of the sweet wine. She put her glass down on the counter. Dylan quickly pulled out a coaster and put it under her glass.

"How's the wine?" Dylan asked.

"Good..." Mackenzie stared at the coaster for a moment. "Good. Um..."

"I'm glad that you showed, Mackenzie...I was actually pretty sure you were going to cancel on me..."

Mackenzie blurted out, "I almost did."

"See..." Dylan laughed. "That's one of the things I really like about you…you're honest. Why don't we go sit down, get comfortable."

"No," Mackenzie said tentatively, then more strongly, "No."

"That's okay. We don't have to sit. I read somewhere that standing is actually better than sitting. Better for the circulation, I think."

"I need to clear something up between us, I think…"

"What's that?"

"I mean…there's the table and the wine and the candles…it's Friday night." Mackenzie had one hand resting on her tote. "This feels kind of like a…date."

Dylan put his glass down slowly on a coaster. "That's because I thought it *was* a date."

"Oh…"

"But you didn't." Dylan stared at her for a moment before he blew out the candles.

*Crap!* She had hurt him. And now Mackenzie was at a rare loss for words as she watched the two twin ribbons of smoke rise from the extinguished candles.

"This is embarrassing." Dylan gulped down his wine and put his glass in the sink.

Both hands clutching the tote, Mackenzie said, "If I'd known that you thought this was a…date…I would never have said yes."

This wasn't the first time he'd embarrassed himself in front of a pretty woman he liked, but in this case, with Mackenzie, it stung just a little bit more than usual.

"I need to check on the salmon," Dylan said.

How she had managed to land on the defensive in this scenario, Mackenzie couldn't figure out…but on the defensive, she was. She followed Dylan to the outdoor kitchen. She sat down on the very edge of a built-in bench; Dylan pushed open the lid of the grill a bit harder than he normally would.

"The salmon looks good," Mackenzie said for lack of anything more helpful to say.

Dylan flipped the salmon steaks over, seasoned them and then shut the lid tightly. Mackenzie felt like a grade-A heel; all she wanted to do now was to smooth things over with Dylan and to get the heck out of Dodge.

"Why would you think this was a date, Dylan?" Guilty, Mackenzie switched from contrite to accusatory.

"Just forget it, Mackenzie." Dylan started to walk back to the house. But then he stopped. "No. You know what? *Don't* forget it. Why *wouldn't* you think this was a date?"

"Because…you're *that*…" Mackenzie waved her hand up and down. "And I'm *this*…I'm not your type."

Dylan sat down on a bench across from her. "How do you know what my type is, Mackenzie?"

"Christa? Jenna? Tall, blonde, skinny." Mackenzie held up three fingers. "And, me? Short, chubby, brunette. Not exactly rocket science."

"You forgot pretty…"

Mackenzie held up a fourth finger. "Pretty goes without saying."

"No," Dylan clarified. "I meant *you*. I think *you're* pretty. And funny and sweet and a really great mom to Hope."

Mackenzie crossed her legs and crossed her arms protectively in front of her body.

Dylan continued, "You know…Jenna and I both loved to surf. And I managed to sustain a relationship built on a mutual love for surfing for nearly a year. You and I have a child together…"

Now Dylan had her full attention.

"And I look at you and I look at Hope…and I think…

maybe I have a chance at what Uncle Bill and Aunt Gerri had together."

"You can't force a family." Mackenzie pulled her sleeves down over her hands and recrossed her arms.

"No, you can't. But you can try to build one." Dylan leaned forward, forearms resting on his thighs. "This doesn't have anything to do with *my* type, does it? That's just an excuse. This has to do with the fact that I'm not *your* type, right?"

"My friend Rayna says that you actually *have* to date to have a type…and I don't. Date, I mean."

"I know. Hope told me. Your friend set you up with a socialist three years ago?"

"He was a *social* worker. A very nice *social* worker. You and Hope certainly cover a lot of subjects, don't you?"

"She likes to talk to me. I like to listen. But let's not get off topic here. I like you, Mackenzie. I want to spend more time with you. And I get that I'm not the obvious choice for you because I don't have a five-page *community service* section on my résumé…but you've gotta admit, I'm a changed man."

Mackenzie thought about Dylan at Pegasus, mucking out stalls, caring for the elderly horses and bonding with the kids. Mackenzie thought of Dylan with Hope; how sweet and kind and patient he was with her. Hope loved him.

Mackenzie held up her pointer finger and her thumb an inch apart. "You've got about this much community service street cred."

The timer next to the grill buzzed. Dylan checked the fish and then pulled them off the grill.

"Come on! Just look at these bad boys." Dylan showed her the steaks. "I can't believe you're really going to let them go to waste."

Mackenzie tugged at the front of her jersey; he had gone to some trouble to make her a healthy meal. "I didn't dress right…"

"Hey—" Dylan sensed that Mackenzie was caving "—if that's the only thing holding you back from hanging out with me tonight, then I'll change. And we can eat out here."

The salmon and broccoli did smell really good. And she *was* really hungry.

"And let's be honest." Dylan's dimples appeared. He was teasing her. "You think I'm sexy when I cook, right?"

"I'll admit…that I *like* a man who can cook."

"See there?" Dylan grinned at her triumphantly. "We can *build* on that!"

Good as his word, Dylan had changed into shorts and a short-sleeved polo, and they dined outside with the ocean as their view. Once Mackenzie stopped focusing on the "date" aspect of the evening and just focused on Dylan, she started to relax and have a good time. They laughed as much as they talked. And there was never a lull in the conversation. They reminisced about their childhood. They talked about Hope and her future aspirations. They talked baseball and surfing and cupcakes. Mackenzie couldn't believe it, but she was sad when the clock on her phone flipped over to nine.

"It's not too late…how about a short walk on the beach? Work off some of this dinner?" Dylan leaned against the island while Mackenzie loaded the last dish in the dishwasher.

"I wish I could…but I've got an early morning at the bakery." Then she surprised herself by adding, "Can I take a rain check?"

From the look on his face, she had surprised Dylan, as well. "Sure."

Mackenzie slipped her tote onto her shoulder and Dylan walked her to the door. They walked down to her car together; Mackenzie pulled her keys out and unlocked the car door. Not wanting to linger in that uncomfortable "end of the night, should I go for the kiss?" moment, Mackenzie wrapped her arms around Dylan's waist, hugged him quickly and then stepped back.

"Thank you…I'm glad that I decided not to go home early…"

Dylan rocked back on his heels. "That's very flattering, thank you."

Mackenzie felt an internal cringe. "That didn't come out right."

"That's okay, Mackenzie." Dylan reached out and opened her car door. "I was just teasing you."

Mackenzie climbed behind the wheel and Dylan closed the door firmly behind her. He tapped on the window so she would roll it down.

Hands resting on the door, Dylan asked, "How 'bout we fill that rain check tomorrow? Say, around seven? We can order in, watch a movie."

"Okay." Mackenzie nodded. She had just accepted a second date with Dylan without one millisecond of hesitation.

"Don't back out," Dylan said.

"I won't…" Mackenzie cranked the engine. "Good night, Dylan."

Dylan nodded his head goodbye as she rolled up the window, shifted into gear and pulled out slowly onto the darkened street. She felt odd driving away from his house—like something significant had just happened to her but she wasn't exactly sure *what*. And, even the next day, as she moved through normal business at the bakery, she still wasn't quite sure what had happened the night before. Dylan hadn't made his thought process a secret: he wanted to see if there was a chance for the two of them, along with Hope, to become a family. That thought had never crossed her mind. But now…was Dylan onto something? *Could* they be a family? If it worked, wouldn't that be the best thing for Hope?

"You're okay to close up, Molly?" Mackenzie untied her apron and lifted it over her head.

"In my sleep, little one." Molly continued to wipe down one of the café tables near the front of the small bakery.

Mackenzie boxed up two of the best-looking giant cupcakes in the case, and gave Molly a kiss on the cheek before she headed out. It was rare that she left the bakery early on a Saturday night, but for once she didn't feel guilty. She felt *anticipation*. She had caught herself thinking about Dylan off and on all day. That just didn't *happen* to her. She had never had a really big crush or even fallen in love, not the way she had seen her friends do—the head-over-heels, can't-sleep, can't-eat, can't-talk-about-anything-else kind of love. In fact, she couldn't remember ever feeling *lust* for anyone before. She had felt a very strong affection for her college boyfriend, but her inability to commit to *Star Trek* had ultimately ended their three-year relationship.

When Hope was born, her entire focus, and all of her love, was aimed at her. She didn't care about dating or romance or marriage. She had Hope. That was enough. It wasn't until Hope was in elementary school that Mackenzie started to think that there might be something missing in her life: intimacy. Romance. *Sex*. But then Hope was diagnosed with ALL and thoughts of a relationship disappeared.

"Wear your hair down this time…" Rayna was on speakerphone.

"You're right. My hair does look good down."

"Are you going to wear the purple shirt?"

"Uh-uh…no. We're walking on the beach, Ray. I can just dress like me."

"Okay…but promise me you'll wear something smaller than extra-extra large! Give the poor man *something* to look at…"

"Bye, Ray!"

"Call me later!"

Unlike the night before, Mackenzie took a little extra time getting ready. She made sure that her long-sleeved V-neck shirt didn't have any stains and she rummaged through her drawers to find a newer pair of jeans. She tried on several pairs and finally selected the jeans that made her J.Lo booty look the best. She let her hair air-dry, leaving it thick and long and falling down her back. She had to admit, she did have beautiful hair. She dug through her messy bathroom drawer and fished out an old tube of mascara from the back. The mascara looked crusty and the brush brittle, so she gave up on that idea. But she did find a tube of lip gloss. Teeth thoroughly brushed for an extra couple of minutes, followed by a long gargle of mouthwash, Mackenzie applied lip gloss and headed out the door. This time when she left the house, there wasn't any confusion about the night. She knew that this was a *date*, and she couldn't wait to see what the night would bring.

## Chapter Nine

She actually felt nervous at the thought of seeing Dylan. She had called Hope to say good-night and now she was standing outside his door, holding her cupcake offering. At some point, a flip had been switched and *just Dylan* had suddenly become *Dylan*. When Dylan opened the door, she thrust the box at him.

"Here."

Dylan pulled one long-stem lavender rose from behind his back and held it out for her. "For you."

Pleased and surprised by the romantic gesture, Mackenzie exchanged the cupcakes for the rose. She lifted the rose up to her nose and breathed in the strong, sweet scent.

"Thank you," she said with a small smile.

"You must've read my mind." Dylan stepped back so she could come inside. "I was craving your cupcakes today."

When they reached the kitchen, Dylan immediately opened the box and grabbed a cupcake.

"Are they both for me, or do I need to share?" Dylan removed the wrapper from the first cupcake and took a large bite.

"They're for you…"

"Hmm…always incredible." Dylan started in on the second cupcake. "I just realized, I've never even bothered to ask you how you got into the cupcake business in the first place."

Mackenzie crossed her arms protectively in front of her, those old, never-forgotten feelings of defensiveness shooting to the surface. "A lot of people ask me that. I always think that there's a built-in insult in there…like they're really asking why a woman with a weight problem would own a bakery…"

Dylan looked at her as if she had lost her mind. "But… that's not what *I* meant."

Ill at ease, Mackenzie tightened her arms around her body. "I'm sorry. Sometimes that old stuff creeps up out of nowhere and flies out of my mouth before I can stop it. Do you ever wish you had a rewind button on your mouth?"

"All the time." Dylan finished the cupcake and put the box in the recycling bin. "And can we just clarify something right now? I happen to think that you're a beautiful woman. Okay?"

"Okay." Mackenzie nodded.

"And I really like it when you wear your hair down like that."

"Thank you." Mackenzie uncrossed her arms. "Do you still want to hear about the bakery?"

"Of course."

"You remember that my mom and I used to bake cupcakes together before she died."

Dylan nodded as she continued, "I remember her always talking about opening up a cupcake shop, but she never got the chance to do it. When I got older, making cupcakes always made me feel happy, and for some odd reason, when I work with sugar and butter, I don't want to *eat* it." Mackenzie smiled a self-effacing smile. "So, when Dad saw me floundering after high school, he offered to send me to school to get my associate's in baking and pastry arts, which then led to a bachelor's degree in bakery and pastry arts management."

"And the bakery?"

"Dad's idea. He made the initial investment, but I'm not gonna sugarcoat it…no pun intended…it's been really tough being a single parent and running a business. After Hope's diagnosis…" Mackenzie paused before she confessed something to Dylan that only Ray knew. "I seriously considered closing. But I have employees to think about…"

"I think you're a really strong woman, Mackenzie. I know how hard it is to run a business."

Mackenzie pulled a small photo album out of her tote. "I brought something for you to look at."

"What's that?" Dylan took the album, flipped to the first page.

Once Dylan realized it was a photo album full of Hope pictures, he slid onto a stool to get more comfortable while he looked at it.

"Look how tiny she was!" Dylan stared at Hope's first baby picture. "'Hope Virginia Brand, 6 pounds 4 ounces, born 3:13 a.m., August 20.'"

"She was an early-morning baby."

"How come there aren't any pictures of you pregnant?"

"Are you kidding me? I would have killed someone if they tried to take my picture when I was pregnant! But, you know, Hope is the reason why I finally lost the weight…"

"How so?" Dylan flipped to the next page.

"After she was born, I knew that I had to get healthy. I

worked really hard to lose the baby weight and then I just kept on losing. The fact that I was doing it for both of us made it easier somehow."

"I would have liked to see you pregnant," Dylan said. "I wish I had been able to be there when Hope was born."

The photo album chronicled Hope's childhood. A childhood he had missed. The little girl in these pictures was lost to him, and a feeling of loss and sadness hit him out of the blue. Dylan used his thumb and forefinger to rub unexpected tears out of his eyes and then he pinched the bridge of his nose to stop more tears from forming.

Wide-eyed, temporarily struck dumb, Mackenzie hadn't expected this reaction from Dylan. When she had played the "photo album scene" over in her mind, she had imagined them laughing and smiling and talking about Hope. Instead, she saw grief. Not knowing what else she could do for him, Mackenzie wrapped her arms around Dylan's shoulders. She hugged him so tightly that the muscles in her arms started to shake. He sat, like a rock, still pinching the bridge of his nose. The sorrow that Dylan felt over having missed his daughter's life was palpable and profound. And, ultimately, she was the one to blame.

"I'm sorry," Mackenzie repeated over and over again. "I'm so sorry."

Dylan turned to her, reached for her and enveloped her in his arms. They clutched each other tightly, their arms entangled, their chests pressed together, their thighs touching. Without warning, Mackenzie's own guilt, her own sorrow and her own feelings of regret overwhelmed her.

"I'm so sorry…" Her tears were absorbed by the material of his shirt.

Dylan pulled back, caught her face between his hands and shook his head.

"Mackenzie…" Dylan wiped her fresh tears away with his thumbs, still holding her face in his hands. "It's okay."

Their eyes locked. And Mackenzie couldn't have looked away if she had the will to do it. Dylan's eyes were naked, raw, unshielded windows into his soul. She continued to stare into his eyes as he moved his thumb sensually over her lower lip. Then his mouth was on hers, without pretense, without warning. Dylan's kiss was soft, tentative, gentle, at first. Then demanding, possessive, sensual. He tasted like sugar; he slipped his tongue past her lips, pulled her body more tightly into his body. Her leg muscles turned to Jell-O; her breathing was quick and shallow. Dylan's arm cradled her back, his fingers fanned out between her shoulders. He kissed her again and again, going a little bit further, taking a little bit more. And then it happened to her. From somewhere deep inside her, untapped and neglected, Mackenzie felt *desire*. Like tiny electrical-shock waves sent tingling and pulsing to the core of her body. Intuitively, Mackenzie pressed her groin into Dylan's… seeking…

The noise Dylan made in the back of his throat struck a primitive chord. And the feel of his arousal, rock hard, thick, searching…made her feel crazy inside. Out of control. She wanted to rip off her jeans, right there in the kitchen, and demand that Dylan use his body to put her out of this new, foreign, *torturous* misery. Mackenzie pushed back against his arm, pushed her hands against his chest. She had to put some distance between them before she let her body's driving needs overrun her reason.

Dylan's arms opened and they both took a step back. Chests rising and falling, desire still sparking in both of their eyes, they were silent. Stunned by what had just happened and uncertain of their next move. Mackenzie touched her fingers to her lips. She had never been kissed like that before; she thought those kind of kisses were for other women. Not her.

"I need to go to the bathroom," Mackenzie blurted out.

Dylan resisted the urge to adjust himself. "Down the hall—second door on the right."

Mackenzie headed to the downstairs bathroom and Dylan chose to head upstairs to the third-floor master bedroom. He took the stairs two at a time; he waited until he had reached his bedroom before he gave in to the need to make the necessary adjustments.

*What the hell just happened?*

Mackenzie had made him nuts: the sensual curves of her womanly body. The full breasts, the roundness of her hips. The way her hair smelled, the feel of her soft lips… the taste of her…it all drove him wild. And he'd wanted to take her right there on the kitchen floor; *would have* taken her, if she had only given him the green light. Dylan sat down on the edge of his bed; he needed some time to cool off before he went back downstairs. If he didn't, he wouldn't put it past himself to try to talk Mackenzie out of her pants and into his bed.

Mackenzie darted into the bathroom and locked the door.

*What just happened?*

She was shaking, not from being cold, not from fear… from *lust…desire…passion.* The most sensitive part of her body, between her thighs, was *throbbing,* for God's sake! She was…*embarrassed.* And hornier than she'd been since she was pregnant with Hope. She couldn't remember the last time she had wanted a man; she had mentally shut down her sexuality years ago. Eventually, her body had followed. But now? Now her body was turned back on with a vengeance. And she was hot for Dylan Axel. With few good options available to her, Mackenzie sat down on the edge of the tub until she could think of a better plan. What does one do in a situation such as this?

*Run for your life*?

"Mackenzie?"

Dylan's knock on the door startled her, made her jump.

"Are you okay?"

"I'm fine!"

An unconvinced pause and then Dylan said, "Are you sure? You've been in there a long time…"

"I'll be out in a minute!"

Mackenzie splashed cool water on her face, glad now that she hadn't put on mascara. Yes, her eyes were watery, red and puffy…but at least she didn't look like a drowned raccoon.

She pointed at her own reflection. "You are *not* a coward. Just go out there and deal with this head-on!"

Determined to exit stage left as soon as possible, she open the door, marched back into the kitchen and prepared to deliver her excuse.

"I hope you like zinfandel…" Dylan had uncorked a bottle of wine.

"I do." That didn't sound like much of an excuse.

Dylan grabbed the bottle, two glasses and a blanket.

"Let's head down to the beach," he said.

Dylan seemed to know exactly what she needed, exactly how she needed it. And instead of making an excuse, as per the plan, she found herself following Dylan down to the beach. When they reached a good spot on the sand, he spread out the blanket. After they were settled, Dylan poured them both a glass of wine and they touched glasses.

"To first kisses." Dylan made the toast.

"First kisses?" Mackenzie didn't take a drink.

"Yeah…tonight was our first real kiss. I don't remember much from the wedding, but I *do* remember that you wouldn't let me kiss you."

"Oh…I'd forgotten about that." Not sure she wanted to repeat that toast, she took a sip of the wine instead. "Good wine."

Night had fallen and they practically had the beach to themselves. There was a party just kicking in to high gear several houses down, but none of the partygoers had wandered down to their small stretch of beach.

It took a second full glass of wine, but Mackenzie no longer felt the least bit awkward or embarrassed.

"Killer view, Dylan…"

"I like it…" Dylan nodded, his eyes focused straight ahead.

By the third glass, Mackenzie had kicked off her shoes, dug her toes in the sand, and she felt all swirly and dreamy like buttercream frosting atop a cupcake. By the fourth glass, Mackenzie was flat on her back, loose as a goose, admiring the stars.

"You're not going to be able to drive home now," Dylan noted.

"That's true," Mackenzie agreed nonchalantly.

Dylan finished his fourth glass of wine. They had finished the bottle. "And I'm not going to be able to *drive* you home."

"That's also true…"

"So…you'll have to spend the night."

Mackenzie giggled. "And here I thought I was too old for a sleepover."

Mackenzie was obviously three sheets to the wind and he was buzzed. It was time to get off the beach. Dylan helped Mackenzie stand up, helped her get steady on her feet and walked up the stairs behind her just in case she tipped backward. Back in the kitchen, Mackenzie folded her arms and laid her head down on the island.

"Come on…" Dylan said kindly. "I'll get you set up in the spare room."

Dylan made sure she had everything she needed for a comfortable night: new toothbrush, toothpaste, a comfortable bed…privacy. He even brought her the top of his pajamas to wear so she wouldn't have to sleep in her clothes. Languid and carefree from the wine, Mackenzie finished in the bathroom, tossed the decorative pillows onto the floor and rolled herself into bed. She sighed happily and snuggled into the downy pillows. Alone, in the dark, her mind drifted back to Dylan's kisses. Her body undoubtedly wanted more and more and more. But did she?

The next morning, she had the answer to that self-imposed question. Slightly hungover, and a little bit headachy, Mackenzie brushed her teeth and then, still in Dylan's pajama top, she left the guest bedroom. The house was quiet as she headed up to Dylan's third-floor master suite. Other than the unmade, empty bed, the room was spotless. The man really was a total neat freak. Her chronic messiness would drive him nuts! Mackenzie stood in the doorway for a moment, rethinking the soundness of her plan. Perhaps she should just turn around, sprint back to her room and catapult herself back into bed.

And she almost did, but then she heard a toilet flush and Dylan appeared, wearing the bottom half of the pajama set, stripped bare above the waist, hair mussed, scratching his chest hair. He didn't notice her as he walked sleepily back to his bed and flopped backward. Mackenzie, frozen to the spot, had been trying, since she had awakened, to formulate her best pitch line, and she had decided on, *Dylan—would you make love to me?*

"Dylan…?"

Surprised by her voice, Dylan bolted upright. "Geez… you scared the crap out of me, Mackenzie." Dylan collapsed back into his fortress of pillows.

"Sorry…"

"Don't worry about it…" Dylan yawned and stretched.

It took him a minute to focus his eyes and really get a look at Mackenzie. Standing shyly in his doorway, hands in the fig-leaf position, she was filling out his pajama top in a way that made his body stand at attention. He pushed himself into a sitting position and casually pulled the covers over the lower half of his body. He had to force himself not to stare at her legs; Mackenzie had really sexy, curvy legs.

"Are you hungry?" Dylan asked after he cleared his throat.

He needed to get her out of his bedroom. The last thing he wanted to do was go too far too fast and run her off the way he almost did last night.

"No." Mackenzie tugged on the bottom of the pajama top to cover more of her legs. "I mean…yes. I am. But no."

Dylan half smiled, half laughed at her odd response. "Say what?"

Mackenzie twisted her fingers together, losing faith in the sanity of her plan. She had been trying to keep things simple and uncomplicated with Dylan back in her life; what she was going to propose was a first-class ticket to *complicated*.

"Yes, I *am* hungry…but *no*, that's not the reason I'm here. In your bedroom…"

"I'm listening…" Dylan was intrigued…and hopeful. Perhaps Mackenzie didn't need to leave his bedroom after all.

"I was wondering…how you would feel about—" she

shifted weight from one leg to the other "—actually, what I'm trying to ask is…do you want to…make love to me?"

"Yes." Dylan took her up on her offer in record time.

"Yes?" Her voice had jumped an octave.

"Yes." He nodded. "I would…like to make love to you."

The man had said yes, which is what she wanted, right? But now she wished she could press Rewind and take back the offer. This couldn't be a good idea, could it? Sex complicated everything. And this situation was already complicated *enough*.

"Come join me…" Dylan peeled back the covers on the empty side of the bed.

Instead of taking the sane and safe option, she walked slowly toward him.

"You look really good in my pajamas…" It was a genius idea to lend her the top of his favorite pair.

Dylan found Mackenzie's nervous smile endearing. He had been used to women who were sexually confident, even aggressive at times. This was a nice change. When Mackenzie reached the side of the bed, she quickly slid beneath the covers and pulled them up to her chin. The tips of her fingers were white from gripping the covers so tightly.

"Did you know—" Dylan turned on his side, kept his hands to himself "—that most men are really nervous about sleeping with a woman for the first time?"

"Is that true or are you just making that up to make me feel better…?"

"I'm not making it up…it's true."

Mackenzie loosened her death grip on the covers. "Are you nervous now?"

"Yeah," Dylan admitted. "Sure I am…"

"Why?"

"Because…there's a lot pressure on a guy to perform, women just don't get it. We're always worried about are we big enough, are we hard enough, are we going to last? Not to mention the pressure of trying to give a woman *multiple* orgasms when it's hard enough just to figure out how to give her one. And trust me, all guys know that our performance, good or bad, is going to be discussed, and dissected, at length with their friends. I'm telling you…it's a lot of pressure to be on the guy end of things."

His attempt to make Mackenzie feel more comfortable with him must have worked, because she put her arms on top of the covers. They were still pinned tightly to her sides, completely blocking him from her body, but it *was* progress.

Dylan reached over, tucked her hair behind her ear and then lightly rested his hand on her arm. "We don't have to do this, Mackenzie. It's okay to change your mind."

"No!" Mackenzie protested. "I *want* to do it. I'm rusty, okay? And I would think," Mackenzie snapped, "that with all your vast experience, you'd know how to get the ball rolling. Aren't you the one with the bachelor pad and models-slash-actresses prancing about half-naked? I made the first move, why can't you make the—"

Dylan's kiss cut off the rest of her words. She liked the minty taste of his tongue; she liked the masculine smell of his skin—no cologne, just Dylan's natural scent. By the time Dylan ended the kiss, Mackenzie no longer felt like complaining. She wanted less talking and more kissing.

"Here…" Dylan tugged on the covers that were still pinned down with her arms. "Let me get closer to you."

Once he managed to coax the covers out of her control, Dylan pressed his body into hers. She continued to lay on her back, stiff and unmoving, when he wrapped his arm around her and draped his leg over her thigh. Dylan made a pleasurable noise as he nuzzled her neck.

"Aren't we supposed to do this *after*…?"

"Relax…" Dylan whispered near her ear.

*Relax. Relax. Just relax!*

"Open your eyes, Mackenzie…" Dylan was admiring her pretty face.

She opened her eyes; it was embarrassing. She only made love in the dark with her eyes closed. And now Dylan wanted them open?

"You have the most amazing eyes… Have I ever told you that before?"

She shook her head. She liked his eyes, too. In the soft morning light, they looked mossy green with flecks of gold around the irises.

He ran his fingers lightly over her lips. "Soft lips."

Those two simple words were followed by a kiss. Once he started kissing her again, he didn't stop. He seemed to enjoy the taste and the feel of her mouth. And she found herself responding to this gentle seduction. He wasn't in a hurry; he wasn't just going through the motions to get to the end zone as fast as he could. Dylan was making her feel special, beautiful…cherished. At first, she was a passive partner, timid and unsure. But his kisses started to change that and she began to touch his body—the hair on his chest, his biceps.

Dylan forced himself to go slow, take his time. Her touch was so tentative and she was so unsure of her own sexuality that it felt as if he was in bed with a virgin. Her body was so voluptuous, so soft, that all he wanted to do was to get rid of that stupid pajama top so he could feel her breasts. He wanted to hold them, massage them…kiss them. The scent of her hair and the feel of her silky skin were aphrodisiacs to him.

Dylan pressed his hard-on against her body, and that's when she felt it again: that throbbing, yearning sensation between her thighs. The next pleasurable sound she heard was her own. Dylan had slipped his hand into her panties and nudged his fingers between her thighs. When he felt how aroused she was, Dylan whispered into her ear.

"I want to be inside of you, Mackenzie." Dylan's voice had a husky, sexy quality now. "Do you want that, too?"

*"Yes."* Why was he talking so much? "Why are you *talking*?"

## Chapter Ten

Dylan gently guided her onto her back. Her pretty lavender-blue eyes were filled with uncertainty and desire, lips parted, cheeks flushed pink, chest rising and falling quickly. She was…stunning. A goddess. And he couldn't wait to see all of her…to love *all* of her. He reached for the top button of her shirt. But Mackenzie stopped him.

"No. I want to leave it on…"

Dylan was disappointed but respected her wishes. A woman as sexy and beautiful as Mackenzie should be proud of her body, not hide it. He shifted his focus, peeled the covers back, exposing her simple white cotton briefs. He caught her eye as he traced the edge of the panties, starting at the inner part of her thigh up to the outer curve of her hip.

"But we will need to take these off…"

This time Mackenzie nodded. Not in a hurry, Dylan gradually inched the covers down, revealing her thighs, knees, and finally her tightly crossed ankles. Dylan noticed a small white scar on her upper thigh; he ran his finger across it.

"I remember when you got this. You cut your leg on a piece of glass in your father's garage."

Mackenzie nodded. Dylan leaned down, kissed the scar before he began to inch her panties down. He was so methodical and deliberate, dropping sensual kisses on her stomach, on the soft fleshy inner part of her thighs. He wasn't in a rush. She wanted to tell him to *hurry up*, but bit her lip instead.

"Mackenzie…you're stunning." Dylan knelt beside her, her underwear now on the floor.

He was the stunning one. Dylan's body was ripped and lean from pounding the waves. There wasn't an ounce of fat on the man; he was a thing of beauty. Dylan stood up, stripped off his underwear and reached for a condom. Mackenzie pulled the covers up over her body and watched, fascinated, as Dylan rolled the condom on. It was bizarre. Dylan had given her a child, but this was the first time she was seeing *all* of his body. The night they conceived Hope, she had insisted on a completely dark room.

Dylan joined her under the blanket and she was relieved that he got right down to business, covered her body with his. His weight felt good, pressing her down into the mattress. His hard shaft felt good, pressed into her belly. Dylan held her face in his hands, but she kept her eyes squeezed tightly shut.

"Mackenzie…" He said her name so sensually. "I wish you'd open your eyes."

Mackenzie opened her eyes. Why was he so patient when she felt as if she was suffering from a serious case of sexual frustration?

"I care about you, Mackenzie. I always have. And…I don't take what we're about to do lightly…"

Aching, throbbing, frustrated, Mackenzie sunk her fingernails into his shoulders. "Dylan! Stop *talking*!"

Dylan smiled down at her but followed orders. He kissed her and eased himself into her body, slow and controlled until he was fully inside of her. Their bodies completely connected now, Dylan didn't move. He dropped his head down, took a minute to compose himself. He didn't want to disappoint Mackenzie with a super-short performance. Mackenzie squirmed beneath him, begging him with her body to *move*.

"Mackenzie," Dylan whispered roughly. "You're driving me crazy…"

His fingers in her hair, his lips on her lips, Dylan began to move. But, slowly, as if he wanted to savor the moment, as if he didn't want this moment to end too soon. His long, deep strokes were exactly what her body had been craving. She lifted her hips to meet him halfway, to take more of him in.

"Wrap your legs around me." Dylan gently bit down on her earlobe.

She wrapped her legs around him, held on to his biceps. Dylan locked his arms to hold himself above her; he closed his eyes and let her watch him. They were starting to learn each other's bodies. Dylan was less cautious now, less gentle, and more demanding and intense. And she *liked* it. Dylan wrapped his arms tightly around her shoulders, curled himself around her, and drove his body into hers. And then he drove her right off the edge of reason and straight into the arms of ecstasy. All of the tension, all of the anticipation and frustration and *building* gave way to orgasmic ripples pinging pleasure signals all over her body. Her loud, vocal orgasm triggered Dylan's.

He thrust into her one last time, deep and hard, and then groaned loudly.

Dylan's breathing was heavy, his body felt heavy atop hers. He was still between her thighs, where she felt raw and wet. Dylan kissed her on the neck; he kissed her on the lips. He pulled the covers up over their still-connected bodies and held her tightly in his arms as if he sensed that she needed that reassuring pressure. She felt emotions, out of nowhere, surge through her. Dylan had just given her an amazing gift—her first *real* orgasm. After his breathing returned to normal, Dylan propped himself up on one arm so he could look at her.

"Are you okay?"

She nodded, still feeling a bit scandalized by her own behavior. She had never been so…*vocal*…in bed before. But she had to admit, that it had been…*liberating*.

"I should take care of this…" He reached down between them, secured the condom between his fingers, and then slowly pulled out of her.

Dylan returned to the bed quickly, propped himself up on the pillows and opened his arms for her.

"Come here. Let me hold you."

Mackenzie wanted to be close to him; she wanted to be in his arms after the lovemaking they had just shared. Dylan wrapped his arms around her, held her tight and sighed like a satisfied, contented man.

"This is a great way to wake up…" Dylan slid his fingers into her hair, a smile in his voice. "You're a wildcat…"

Mackenzie ran her fingers through his chest hair, smiled but kept quiet.

"I don't think anyone has surprised me the way you just did…" Dylan kissed the top of her head and rubbed her arm. "Hey…what are you doing today?"

"No plans, really. The bakery's closed on Sundays and I don't pick up Hope from her friend's house until four."

"And I already called Pegasus and told them that I wouldn't be there today, so my day is free. Why don't we spend the day together."

"What did you have in mind?"

"Breakfast, for starters."

"Agreed…"

"Then, surfing?"

"Negative."

Dylan laughed. "Okay…the hot tub, then."

"Uh-uh…I don't have a swimsuit."

"Skinny-dipping is encouraged."

"I never negotiate on an empty stomach. Let's eat first and then we'll talk."

Dylan was an organized, clean cook. She would drive him nuts; her bakery was spotless, but when she baked, she was a whirlwind—a *messy* whirlwind.

"You really do have a little OCD thing happening, don't you?" Mackenzie observed Dylan cleaning the counter throughout the cooking process.

"I guess. I just like things to be clean, organized. What's wrong with that?" Dylan twisted the rag dry and then dropped it over the faucet.

"We could never get married," Mackenzie said without thinking.

*Really? You just brought up marriage?*

"Oh, yeah?" Dylan flipped over the pancakes. "Why not?"

"Not that I was suggesting that *I* think that we *should* get married. It was just an observation…"

"You still haven't told me why not…"

"In the hypothetical?"

"If you'd like…" Dylan leaned back against the counter, crossed his arms in front of him.

"You are obviously a neat freak. And I am…*not* a neat freak."

"I know." Dylan smiled at her, set her heart fluttering. "I've seen your office, remember?"

"That's right." Mackenzie nodded. "So…you see my point?"

"No. I don't." Dylan put a stack of pancakes on a plate for her. "I have a maid. Problem solved."

Mackenzie could never imagine her life with a maid, which was yet another difference between them, but she decided to move on to a different subject. Dylan saturated her pancakes in butter and syrup, piled crispy bacon onto her plate and served her hot coffee. He ignored her calorie concerns, citing that everyone should allow themselves to have at least *one* cheat day a week and this was it. His logic, and the fact that he seemed to like a woman with a good appetite, encouraged her to devour the pancakes along with a second helping of bacon.

"I really don't normally eat like this," Mackenzie said, looking guiltily at her near-empty plate.

"Do you want more?" Dylan asked. "There're a couple of pieces of bacon left."

Mackenzie pushed her plate away from her and cringed. "Uh-uh…no. I've eaten too much already."

Dylan had managed to charm her into complacency and all she could think of now was how many calories she had just consumed.

"Hey…" Dylan leaned on his forearm and stared at her face. "Mackenzie…please stop beating yourself up about the food. Okay? Give yourself permission to have a little fun."

After they cleaned up after breakfast, Dylan convinced

her that the next logical step was to step down into his hot tub.

Mackenzie went to the guest room to change into a pair of Dylan's boxer briefs and a T-shirt. She called to check on Hope and then quickly sent Ray an I'm OK text message before she emerged from the room wearing Dylan's makeshift bathing suit.

"I look ridiculous," she complained to Dylan.

Dylan was in his surf trunks, bare to the waist, and barefoot. "Not to me you don't."

Dylan circled behind her and pulled the extra material of the T-shirt toward the back. "Here…let me tie a knot back here or the shirt will float up when you get in the water."

Now standing in front of her, he eyed her appreciatively. "There. Perfect."

Mackenzie looked down. Dylan's adjustment to the outfit pulled the front of the shirt tight over her breasts.

"Was that for my sake or yours?" she asked, half-teasing, half-serious.

"Both…" Dylan wasn't shy about admiring her with his eyes. "Definitely both."

She felt self-conscious walking out to Dylan's hot tub, but once she slipped into the hot, bubbling water, Mackenzie forgot all about her silly outfit. Dylan was right— this was bliss.

*"Aaaaah."* Mackenzie sank down farther into the water.

"Uh-huh…didn't I tell you?" Dylan slid in beside her.

"You did."

Beneath the water, Dylan reached for her hand. Pleased, she intertwined her fingers with his, dropped her head back, closed her eyes and let her mind go blissfully blank. Time moved but they didn't. Not for a while. Not until the sun, beating down on her scalp, finally became too hot to bear. Mackenzie sighed deeply, opened her eyes and moved to the middle of the hot tub. Dylan's interested eyes followed her every move. She leaned back and dipped her hair back into the water so she could cool off her scalp, and to slick her hair back. When she stood up and turned around, Dylan was smiling at her.

"What?" Mackenzie asked. "Why are you grinning at me like a Cheshire cat?"

Dylan's eyes drifted down to her breasts. "Can't I admire you?"

Mackenzie followed his gaze. The wet T-shirt had molded itself to her breasts, leaving nothing to the imagination. Mackenzie immediately sunk down in the water to her neck.

"No…" Dylan shook his head. "You've got to stop doing that."

Dylan was at her side, his arm around her waist; he kissed her as their bodies floated backward toward the side of the hot tub. Dylan lifted her into his arms, spun around and pulled her onto his lap. Then he kissed her again, his tongue taking possession of her mouth, his hand taking possession of her breast. He was already aroused; she could feel it against her thigh.

"When I take you back upstairs, Mackenzie…" Dylan whispered sensually into her ear. "I don't want there to be anything between us this time."

Mackenzie knew that Dylan was referring to the fact that she hadn't let him take off her top when they had made love. Her body wanted Dylan again, and so did she.

"Dylan…" Mackenzie moaned pleasurably into the sun-warmed skin on his neck. "Take me back upstairs…"

After they made love for a third time, Mackenzie took a shower, alone, in the guest bathroom. Dylan offered to share his shower with her, but for some reason, even after all of the lovemaking, a shower seemed somehow too...*intimate*. Mackenzie hurried through her shower, got dressed and made the bed. She tried to arrange the decorative pillows exactly as she had found them but finally gave up.

Dylan was lounging in the den, flipping through TV channels, waiting for her. "What would you like to do with your free afternoon?"

Mackenzie smiled a mischievous smile. "There is something that I'd really like to do."

"What's that?"

Mackenzie's smile widened. "Drive the Corvette."

She thought that Dylan was going to shut her down immediately. To guys like her brother, Jett, and Dylan, their cars were their babies. And they didn't let *anyone* get behind the wheel.

He shocked her when he said, "I'll let you drive her. We can take her down to Ocean Beach Pier. Have you been to the restaurant on that pier?"

Mackenzie shook her head no.

"Have you ever tried fish tacos?"

She wrinkled her nose distastefully. "No..."

"Then today is your lucky day, Mackenzie!"

They gathered their things and then Dylan handed her the keys to his pride and joy. She slid into the driver's seat and wrapped her hands around the steering wheel. As she backed out of the garage, she was half expecting him to have a change of heart and scream for her to stop. It didn't happen. They rolled down the windows, turned on the radio to a classic-rock station and headed to the pier. She wanted to open her up and really test the horsepower under the hood, but she didn't. The last thing she wanted to do was leave even so much as a scratch on a car this valuable. They parked and walked down to the beach. Dylan's phone had been ringing and beeping with texts and emails. He finally just shut his phone off and left it in the car. She didn't ask about who was trying to contact him, but she knew his recent history. He was a single, good-looking guy with deep pockets and a party pad. She didn't doubt his friends, both male and female, were missing one of their regular spots to party at the beach.

They walked side by side, but Mackenzie wasn't ready to hold hands in public. They never stopped talking, that's what she liked about hanging out with Dylan. She wouldn't have thought that they'd have much to say to each other, but they did. He made her laugh; he was silly and goofy and liked to joke around. He'd never really taken life too seriously when they were kids, and he still didn't. He still liked to have fun, and he wanted to take her along for that ride.

"Okay…be honest…" Dylan had just demolished five fish tacos. "You shouldn't have judged, right?"

The Ocean Pier Restaurant was built on the side of the pier. They were sitting at a small table with an incredible view, and Dylan insisted that she, at the very least, take a bite of their famous fish tacos.

Mackenzie chewed the small bite of fish taco thoughtfully.

"Well?" Dylan demanded impatiently. "Awesome, right?"

"It's…pretty good…" Mackenzie said, glad that she had refused the tacos and stuck with an egg-salad sandwich and water. She was still pretty full from breakfast and she couldn't just stop worrying about calories because he had encouraged her to do it. Calorie watching was her normal. Dylan, on the other hand, had been happy to tell her during the car ride that making love to her had left him famished.

"Pretty good?" Dylan acted as if she had just stabbed him in the heart. "You're killing me! These are *legendary*. Try another bite…"

"No!" She pressed her lips together and shook her head. "I wouldn't dream of taking even one more bite away from you…"

"Okay…" He was perfectly happy to polish off the rest by himself. "Are you sure?"

The taco had left a bad taste in her mouth that couldn't be washed away with water alone. She nodded yes while she dug through her tote to find her mints.

They finished their lunch, cleared their table and stepped out onto the pier. Dylan looked around. "Are you up for a walk?"

"Sure," she agreed. They had walked a little ways, when he gave her a curious look. "I thought you liked me."

"I do…"

"Then how come you're so far away?" He offered her his arm.

She took his arm and they strolled together along the pier. When the sun felt a little too strong on her face, the salty mist from the water crashing against the pier seemed to come just at the right time when her skin felt too hot. She couldn't remember the last time she had been to the pier. She had certainly never been here on a date. In this moment, she was content; happy to be walking beside Dylan.

At the end of the pier, Dylan asked, "Do you want to head back or sit down on one of these benches and people watch?"

"People watch, of course."

Like an old comfortable couple, they sat together on the bench. Dylan put his arm behind her shoulder; she leaned in just a little bit closer.

"Do you have the photo album with you? The one from last night?"

Mackenzie put her hand on her tote. "Right here."

"I'd like to finish looking at it."

"Are you sure?"

"I want to know more about our daughter."

*Our daughter.*

Dylan had never used that term before.

Dylan started at the beginning while Mackenzie told him the story behind each picture. Halfway through the album, they came to the pictures that chronicled Hope's cancer journey.

"Her face is so swollen in this picture. She doesn't even look like the same kid," Dylan said. Hope's face was puffy and round, her head completely bald, her eyebrows gone.

"Steroids," Mackenzie explained. "She could never seem to get enough food." Mackenzie pointed to the next picture. "This is when she first got her port put in for chemo. That was a…really bad day."

Dylan flipped through the rest of the photographs and then went back to the first picture—the one taken the day Hope was born.

"You know that I love her now, Mackenzie."

Mackenzie nodded. She did know.

"And, I'm…really worried about her. What if she relapses?"

Mackenzie didn't like to think about that. She put the album in the tote. "Then we fight it. That's all we can do."

They stayed at the pier for another hour; before they headed back to the car, Dylan insisted that he take her to his favorite ice-cream shop, which was famous for its waffle ice-cream sandwich. After the ice cream, Dylan drove them back to his place. Climbing out of the low-slung Corvette, Mackenzie couldn't remember having a better time with a man.

"Do you want to come in for a while? Or do you have to go?"

"I have to go. I pick Hope up at four. School tomorrow."

On the way back to the car, Dylan made her promise to return the favor and let him drive her vintage Chevy the next time they saw each other.

"I had a really good time with you, Mackenzie. And I know this is going to sound kind of strange, because we have Hope, so I *will* be seeing you again…but I want to see you again."

Dylan was leaning against her driver's door. For the whole entire day, right up until this moment, Mackenzie had felt really good about her decision to deepen the connection with Dylan. But now that she was getting ready to return to reality, her life…doubt was starting to creep in fast and loud.

"Why do I get the feeling something just went wrong here?" Dylan asked suspiciously. Mackenzie's body language, the expression on her face, had changed. Her eyes, which had been open and willing, were guarded.

"There's nothing wrong, Dylan," she lied. "It's just time for me to get back to real life."

He hadn't believed the lie. "I think we should make a date right now. How about if the three of us drive out to Aunt Gerri's house next Sunday? She's been asking for both of you."

"Um…let me check my calendar, okay? And I'll get back to you."

"Now, see…I feel like I need to get a commitment out of you…pin you down." Dylan frowned. "It seems like you're already having second thoughts about this weekend. I can feel you backing away from me…"

Mackenzie took a small step back. "I don't think I'm backing away from you…"

"Actually, you just literally *did* back away from me."

Dylan reached out, slipped his fingers through her hair to the nape of her neck and brought her lips to his. He kissed her until he felt her take a step back toward him. And he didn't *stop* kissing her, until she melted into his arms.

"So…" His lips were still so very close to hers. "Do we have a date?"

"You don't play fair, do you?"

"Not when it comes to you." Dylan kissed her again. "Do we have a date?"

"Yes, Dylan." He was a very persuasive kisser. "We have a date."

## Chapter Eleven

"What do you think?" Mackenzie stood in the doorway of her room feeling *naked* in the short-sleeved purple blouse. It was Sunday, and they were scheduled to meet up with Dylan in an hour so they could all go out to his aunt's farm together. She wanted to look presentable, and even though she had been having misgivings about her weekend with Dylan, she wanted to look nice for him, too.

"I picked that out." Hope was a stylish kid. She loved jewelry and accessories; she cut pictures out of fashion magazines and couldn't wait to wear makeup. "You look pretty, Mom."

Mackenzie checked her reflection in the mirror again, tugged on the front of the blouse. It was strange seeing so much of her arms, and they still looked too *round* for her liking, but lately she'd started to think that she needed to force herself out of her baggy-fashion box. There was no doubt in her mind that Dylan's regular compliments had boosted her body image. She still had work to do, but at least she was able to finally cut the tags off this blouse and put it on her body. Mackenzie pointed to her reflection in the mirror.

"You look good," she said, then shut off the bathroom light and headed to the kitchen. She took a quick sip of her strong black coffee before preparing Hope's morning medicine.

"Did you make your bed?" Mackenzie called out to Hope.

She knew that she was never going to be a complete neat freak like Dylan, but she was starting to think that a little more organization wouldn't hurt. In fact, she was very proud of the fact that all their dinner dishes had made it directly into the dishwasher without their typical pit stop to the sink.

"Yeah." Hope showed up looking cute as a bug in a sparkly butterfly T-shirt, cuffed jeans and lavender tennis shoes. "But why'd I have'ta start doing *that* now?"

Mackenzie held out the pills for Hope. "It wouldn't hurt us to be a little neater around here…I made mine, too."

Hope made a face at the pills.

"I know, kiddo. But you gotta take them. Down the hatch."

Mackenzie handed Hope a glass of grape juice, watched her take her pills. When she was done, Mackenzie rinsed out the glass and put it in the dishwasher.

"You feeling okay today?"

"Uh-huh…" Hope nodded.

Mackenzie and Hope loaded into her Chevy and headed toward the bakery. She had agreed to meet Dylan there and she didn't want to be late. During the short trip from their house to the bakery, Mackenzie couldn't seem to get comfortable. She fiddled with the radio, the AC, her seat belt, the neckline of her blouse. She was fidgety and uncomfortable. Anxious. This would be the first time Dylan and she would be seeing each other after their weekend alone. He'd called, but she had made excuses: she was tired, she was working…bad reception, low battery. She just didn't know what to say to him, so it was just easier to say nothing at all. The farther away she got from the weekend, the more she beat herself up for jumping into bed with him. Yes, her body had been deprived in that area for years, but her brain knew better.

And, as often happened with spur-of-the-moment libido-driven decisions, by Monday night, Mackenzie was marinating in full-blown regret. It had been a *terrible* idea to sleep with Dylan. Their focus, their only focus, should have been on Hope—not on each other. She needed to tell Dylan how she felt when they were face-to-face and, hopefully, the two of them could agree to refocus their attention on Hope. If the right moment materialized today, she knew that she needed to have a talk with Dylan.

Dylan arrived at the parking lot behind the bakery ahead of schedule. He was usually early. While he was waiting for Mackenzie and Hope, he decided to try his attorney's private number. He was surprised when Ben actually answered.

"Hey, Ben! I was planning on leaving you a message."

"Do you want me to hang up?" Ben asked.

"No." Dylan laughed. "This is better."

"What can I do for you, Dylan?"

"I had a chance to look over the papers you emailed. Everything looks good, exactly as we discussed."

"That's what I like to hear. Just send a signed copy to the office and we'll have them in the mail to the mother this week."

"Actually…that's what I was calling you about. I'd like to hold off on sending the papers. Just for a little bit."

"May I ask why?"

"I'm hoping that we can work some of this stuff out on our own. So far, things have been pretty cordial between us. But if Mackenzie gets these papers now, I think she'll go ballistic and turn this into World War Three."

"I see. Well, ultimately, it's your decision." Ben paused for a moment of thought. "Why don't we do this…send over a signed copy and we'll hang on to the papers until you're ready to pull the trigger. How does that sound?"

Dylan saw Mackenzie's Chevy pulling into the parking lot and wanted to get off the phone quickly. "That sounds like a plan, Ben. Thanks for picking up on a weekend."

"Billable hours, my friend," Ben said jokingly. "Billable hours."

Hope hugged him hello and Mackenzie greeted him by handing him the keys to her Chevy. He didn't have a car with a backseat, so Mackenzie volunteered her car. And since he had let her drive his Corvette, it was his turn to drive her Chevy. The vintage Chevy had a bench seat in front big enough to fit all three of them. He was behind the wheel, Mackenzie was in the seat by the passenger door and Hope was seated between them. Dylan had the distinct feeling that Mackenzie was glad to put some distance between them in the car, especially since she had been giving him the cold shoulder all week. He'd thought they'd had a great weekend together. *She* came to *his* room. Not the other way around. But he'd blown off enough women when he was in his twenties to know when it was happening to him. He just didn't understand *why*. Luckily, they had Hope to fill in the large gaps in conversation between them.

"See this fence right here, Hope? All of this land belongs to my aunt." Dylan slowed down so Hope could see the farm.

Hope leaned forward, her eyes large. "Whoa…I wish she had horses still!"

Dylan made the turn onto the main driveway. He braked and stared at the For Sale sign posted at the entrance.

"I didn't know the farm was for sale," Mackenzie said.

"Neither did I." Dylan's forehead wrinkled pensively before he slowly let off the brake and headed toward the farmhouse.

Mackenzie saw the empty pastures and the weathered farmhouse in the distance and felt the memories stir inside of her. She had been Hope's age the last time she had seen this farm. Her mother had died the year before; Dylan had just lost his mother. Dylan's birthday party that year, the first without his mother, was one of those memories that had always stuck out in her mind when she thought of her childhood. Aunt Gerri and Uncle Bill had gone out of their way to make sure Dylan had the best birthday that he could possibly have. There was cake and presents and horseback rides and games. She remembered having a really good time; she remembered that Dylan's aunt had let her help in the kitchen. She also remembered that Dylan's smile, the entire day, had always been forced. The smile had never reached his eyes.

Dylan honked the horn and then shut off the engine. A few minutes later, Aunt Gerri swung open the door and came out onto the porch.

"There she is," Dylan said proudly.

Aunt Gerri waved both hands in the air, her bright blue eyes shining with a welcoming smile on her round face.

"Oh, my goodness! Let me look at you!" His aunt held

out her arms to Hope. "You're just the prettiest little girl I've seen in my whole entire life."

Unlike when Hope had met him, she didn't hesitate to hug his aunt straight away.

"And Mackenzie! I'm so glad to see you again."

Even though he wanted immediately to start questioning his aunt about the For Sale sign, he forced himself to wait. Aunt Gerri was brimming with things to say while she gave Mackenzie and Hope the tour of the place. Dylan followed behind them, biding his time until he could ask her about the sign.

"Here's a picture of Bill and me at our fiftieth wedding anniversary." Aunt Gerri stopped in front of a large portrait hanging in the formal living room. "It wasn't too long after this picture was taken that we found out he was sick."

They finished the tour in the front room. The last time he was in this room, he had told his aunt about Hope. Now Hope was here, admiring his aunt's year-round Christmas tree. He waited while his aunt showed Hope and Mackenzie her favorite ornaments. While he waited, he straightened the stacks of sheet music on top of the organ. And, then he got tired of waiting.

"Aunt Gerri...?"

"Hmm?" His aunt was showing Hope her favorite Olive Oyl ornament.

"There's a For Sale sign at the gate. When did you decide to sell?"

His aunt hung Olive Oyl back in her place. "Oh, a couple of weeks ago, I suppose."

Dylan breathed in deeply and then sighed. He'd been feeling anxious ever since he'd seen the sign. His aunt had always owned this farm, for as long as he could remember. It was a touchstone for him. It had always been there if he needed it.

"I didn't even know you were thinking about it…"

Aunt Gerri gestured for Hope and Mackenzie to have a seat. To Dylan she said, "Why do you look so surprised, Dylan? You had to know this would happen eventually."

"I don't know…" Dylan sat down in his grandmother's rocking chair. "I suppose I didn't think it would ever happen. Not really. I thought Sarah or Mary would want the property…"

"No," Gerri said of her daughters. "They both have big-time careers back East. They've never wanted the responsibility of the farm. None of you did…" His aunt smiled a wistful smile. "It's just time, I suppose. It's been time, really. Once Bill was gone, the place was never the same. And I want to be closer to town so I can see my friends. I want to be closer to my church. And I try to think about what Bill would want me to do. You know, your uncle was a black-and-white person, not an in-between person. I don't think he'd like to see what we worked so hard to build together shrink bit by bit until there's nothing left but this house. Better to let it go now. And you've got to remember, Dylan, this land is my retirement."

Sometimes the truth did hurt, Dylan thought. To his aunt, he said, "I'm just sad to see it go."

"I know you are, hon. You never were one for change. But unless you're in the market for a farm, it's got to be sold."

"You should buy it, Dylan!" Hope exclaimed, her face very hopeful. Dylan could see the dreams of horses dancing in her blue-violet eyes.

Dylan shook his head with a laugh. "Sorry, Hope. That's not gonna happen."

Hope jumped up from her seat, brimming with enthusiasm. She talked with her hands and her mouth. "But we could fix up the barn and rent out the stalls. We could give riding lessons out here and clinics and I could have my own horse…"

"I knew that was coming," Mackenzie interjected.

"And when I become a hippo-therapist, I could have my business here!"

"Now what do you want to be when you grow up? A hippa-what?" Dylan knew his aunt and she was getting a kick out of Hope's heartfelt plea.

That question was all the encouragement Hope needed. She sat down in the rocking chair next to Aunt Gerri's and told her all about her future plans. Mackenzie and Dylan's eyes caught occasionally while Hope and his aunt engrossed themselves in a conversation built for two. It reminded Dylan of a Norman Rockwell picture, the two of them together, sitting in rocking chairs in a well-lived-in farmhouse. His aunt had two daughters, both professionals, both living in big cities; his cousins had favored Uncle Bill. But his Hope? She favored his aunt to a T. And, right from the word *go*, they had hit it off, just as one would expect two peas in a pod to do.

"Well…you've definitely got your dad's imagination, that's for sure," Aunt Gerri said. Aunt Gerri didn't notice it, but there was a moment of discomfort between the three of them. No one had called him Hope's dad yet. "Do you remember, Dylan? You tried to convince Bill to turn one of the pastures into a skateboard park. He tried and tried, bless his heart," she said to Mackenzie and Hope. "I remember Bill coming to bed one night so impressed by Dylan. He said that he actually came up with a plan to charge kids so the skateboard park would pay for itself."

"I'd forgotten about that…" Dylan said.

"How about a tour of the farm, Hope?" Aunt Gerri asked. Dylan had a feeling she was just looking for an excuse to get the old golf cart out of storage.

Hope was more than willing to take a tour with his aunt. Aunt Gerri grabbed her keys and they all headed outside. Mackenzie watched Hope load into his aunt's golf cart, while Dylan sat down on the front-porch swing.

"If I know my aunt, they're going to be gone for a while. Come over here and keep me company."

Mackenzie waited until the golf cart disappeared from view before she took him up on his offer. She had wanted to catch Dylan alone, have a chance to set things straight between them. But now that she *did* have him alone, she wasn't exactly sure what she wanted to say to him.

"I'm actually glad that we have a chance to talk to each other without an audience."

Mackenzie nodded, tugged on the short sleeves of her blouse.

"I like that color on you, Mackenzie." Dylan complimented her blouse. "It matches your eyes."

Mackenzie didn't look at Dylan when she said thank-you.

"I wanted to tell you when I first saw you, but I was afraid that you'd be upset with me for complimenting you in front of Hope…"

When Mackenzie didn't say anything, Dylan continued, "And I guess I'm kind of confused here, Mackenzie. I thought we had a good time together last weekend. I know *I* did. I had a better time just hanging out with you than I've had with anyone else in a really long time."

Mackenzie examined her hands instead of returning his gaze. "I had a really good time, too, Dylan."

"Then what's wrong? You haven't been returning my phone calls. When I can get you on the phone, you're always rushing me off. Do you regret what happened between us? Is that it? Do you wish that we hadn't—" Dylan lowered his voice even though there wasn't a soul in sight "—made love?"

Mackenzie glanced at him. "I've been beating myself up about that all week…"

"Well…" Dylan gave a small shake of his head, looked off into the distance. "I'm really sorry you feel that way."

"This isn't about you, Dylan. It's not even about me. It's about Hope. Don't you think I've been lonely? Don't you think I'd like to have someone in my life? I would. But I can't even think about that now. All my energy has to be focused on getting Hope permanently well and keeping my business open. That's it." Mackenzie shook her head. "What happened between us last weekend…I take full responsibility for how far things went."

"Jesus…don't confess to me like you committed a crime! I don't regret what happened between us, either. I actually have some pretty strong feelings for you, Mackenzie."

And he did. Right there, on his aunt's porch, swinging on the porch swing with Mackenzie felt right. She was that missing piece of the puzzle, the one that completed the picture of his life. And from her demeanor…from her body language…it wasn't hard to read that his feelings weren't exactly returned.

"You don't have to say that," she said in a small, tense voice.

"Why shouldn't I say it, Mackenzie? It's the truth. And, from where I sit, we've got nothing standing in our way. You're single. I'm single. We already have a child together. Give me one good reason why we shouldn't *try* to be a family."

Mackenzie didn't feel as if she had one good reason. She felt as if she had a hundred good reasons. But at the core of all her reasons was Hope. What would it do to Hope if they tried to be a family and failed? She was closer to Hope than she had ever been to any human being in her life. And she knew, without a doubt, that Hope couldn't handle that kind of disappointment. Not right now.

Mackenzie stood up and moved to the railing. Putting some distance between them seemed like a good idea.

"If you don't have feelings for me, Mackenzie…that's one thing. But if you're just shutting me down because you're afraid…"

"*Of course* I'm afraid," Mackenzie snapped at him. "It's taken me a long time to get traction after Hope was diagnosed, okay? But I still feel like I've built a matchstick house…like the slightest move could make the whole thing burst into flames. I'm always dreading the next test results, always dreading the next medical bill…"

"But I told you that I want to help you with that," Dylan said.

The comment about the medical bills had just slipped out. Dylan had offered since the beginning to pay child support. He'd offered to help her with medical expenses. But she had always refused. For her, taking money from Dylan was like opening up yet another can of worms. There were a lot of legal strings that could come with that money…visitation, joint custody…and she just couldn't bring herself to wade into those waters just yet. The minute they sat down to establish paternity and child support, Dylan would have rights and she couldn't guarantee what he would do with them. She would have to consult him about educational and medical decisions. She had always prided herself on being able to care for Hope on her own. She had always prided herself on being a strong, successful single parent. The fact that change was already fraying the edges of her life only made her want to cling to how things "were" even more.

"I know you did," Mackenzie said more calmly. "And maybe that's what will happen…eventually. But for now, why can't we just take everything one day at a time?"

"I don't have any problem with taking things slow. But you've gotta be straight with me, Mackenzie. Is the only thing you think about what happened between us last weekend is that it was a mistake?"

Mackenzie rejoined Dylan on the swing.

"No. That's not what I think. What I think is that I have a responsibility as Hope's mom to think before I move. I owe that to her. And last weekend I lost sight of that."

She didn't want to hurt Dylan. She didn't. In her heart, she knew that she had never felt for another man what she had been feeling for Dylan this last week apart. And it scared her. She hadn't allowed herself to become vulnerable to someone in a long time and she wasn't so sure she had it in her to do it now.

"I want to be in a relationship, Dylan," Mackenzie confessed. "Not just for me. But for Hope. When she was younger, it didn't matter as much…now that she's old enough to have friends with two parents, she knows what she's missing…and I think…she wants a family. I wasn't able to admit it to myself for a long time because I wanted to be enough. I didn't want to think that I had made a mistake for all of us all those years ago. But I think…I know… that's why she wanted to find you in the first place."

"I want to try for that, too…"

"But what if we can't make it work between us? What would that do to Hope?"

"What if we *can* make it work?" Dylan answered her question with a question.

"If you're not closing the door on us…"

"I'm not." Mackenzie put her hand on his.

"Then we'll take it real slow… You're both worth the wait."

When Mackenzie saw Aunt Gerri's golf cart in the distance, she pulled her hand back from his.

"I think that if we always put Hope's best interests first, everything else will fall into place…" Mackenzie stood up and waved to Hope. She didn't look at him when she asked, "So, we have a deal?"

"Yes." Dylan stood up and stood next to her. He was close, but not *too* close. "We have a deal."

## Chapter Twelve

Mackenzie came home late Wednesday night feeling worn-out and tired from the day. Her main goal was to spend some time with Hope, make sure the little girl was caught up on her homework and then go to bed.

"Hey, Mackenzie." Charlie was sitting on her love seat. The TV was on, but the sound was on Mute.

"Hey…" Mackenzie pulled her key out of the door and closed it behind her. She dropped her bag on the floor next to the door and slumped into a chair.

"You look tired."

Mackenzie dropped her head into her hand. "I am… We've had a ton of responses from the ad we ran in the trade magazine. A lot of special orders. This entire week is going to be crazy and Hope has chemo this Friday—" Mackenzie sighed "—so this weekend is going to be tough." Mackenzie looked toward Hope's bedroom. "Is she still working on her homework?"

"No," Charlie said quietly, shaking her head. "She went to bed early."

Mackenzie pushed herself up, looked at her watch. Hope usually fought going to sleep. She always wanted to stay up later than her official bedtime. "Is she sick?"

"She said that she was really tired and wanted to go to bed." Charlie stood up. "I've got an early morning tomorrow, Mackenzie, so I'm going to head home, okay?"

Mackenzie stood up, her mind on her daughter. She hugged Charlie. "Thanks for watching her."

"You know I love to hang with Hope." Charlie opened the door. Offhandedly, she said, "Oh…I put your mail on the kitchen counter."

Mackenzie locked and dead-bolted the door behind Charlie, grabbed the mail off the counter and went to check on Hope. Lately she had been getting a sickening feeling in her gut. Hope just hadn't been herself for a couple of days. Mackenzie sat down on the side of Hope's bed, ran her hand gently over Hope's head. She felt her forehead with her wrist. It was cool. Hope cracked open her eyes.

"Hi, Mom," she said groggily.

"Hi, kiddo. Are you feeling okay?"

Hope reached out for her mom's hand. "I'm tired."

"Are you having any other symptoms? Are you achy? Do you have a sore throat?"

Hope shook her head, pressed her face into the pillow. "Not really. Just tired."

Concerned, Mackenzie gently rubbed her daughter's back. "I think we should take you to the doctor tomorrow…"

Hope's eyes opened, she turned slightly. "No…" she begged. "Mom…we're going to finish making our birdhouses tomorrow in art class and then we get to hang them up around school! I'm already going to the doctor on *Friday*!"

Mackenzie stared down into her daughter's pleading eyes; it broke her heart that Hope had already missed out on so much after she was first diagnosed. So, against her better judgment, she agreed to let Hope go to school and wait until Friday to see the doctor as planned.

Mackenzie kissed her daughter on the forehead, stood up. "Okay, kiddo. Get some rest. If anything changes, you come get me, okay? I'll see you in the morning."

Mackenzie paused in the doorway for a second or two, watching her daughter drift back to sleep, before she quietly closed the door. Hope's blood would be tested on Friday. Maybe this was nothing to worry about, but she had learned from terrible experience not to minimize symptoms anymore.

She kicked off her shoes and flopped backward onto her pillows. She rested the pile of mail on her stomach, wanting to delay contact, for just a little while longer, with the stack of envelopes that had to be at least fifty percent medical bills. With a long, tired sigh, Mackenzie sat up and started to sift slowly through the mail. The second envelope had bright red paper showing through the cellophane. She ripped open the envelope, looked at the dollar amount and then started a separate "delinquent" medical bill pile. One by one, she separated the mail. As the medical bill pile grew in size, so did her anxiety. It was a daily ritual, with only a brief respite on Sundays. The mail, with its constant stream of bad news, now regularly triggered the feeling that she was slowly being buried alive in quicksand.

Mackenzie was glad to reach the last envelope in the pile; there wasn't any angry red paper glaring at her from behind the cellophane. But once she looked closer at the return address, her psyche shifted.

"Levine, Ernest and Seeger, PA"

She ripped the thick envelope open and pulled out the papers within. She didn't have to read the papers to surmise who had sent them. The only person in her life with a reason to retain an attorney was Dylan. And during their lengthy, private, *supposedly* open and *honest* conversation on Sunday, Dylan had failed to mention that his *attorney* would be contacting her.

Mackenzie began to read quickly through the lengthy documents. With each new written "demand" set forth by Dylan and his attorney, her shaky fingers tightened on the pages, crumpling the edges of the crisp linen paper.

She sat on the edge of the bed, stunned and still. Her brain was on fire: *Why* hadn't she seen this freight train coming?

Mackenzie slammed the papers down on her bed and picked up her phone. She scrolled through her recent-call list and stared hard at Dylan's name. She was tempted to call him right now; verbally blast him *right now*. But she didn't. She closed her eyes and tried to calm her body down: her brain, her heartbeat, her blood pressure. They were all out of control. As much as she wanted to confront Dylan about these papers, she didn't want to give him the advantage by being the out-of-control emotional one on the phone.

Instead of calling Dylan, Mackenzie got herself ready for bed. She doubted that she was going to get much sleep, but she knew she had to try. *This week* was not the week to be ragged from sleep deprivation. Now more than ever, she needed to be on her A game. Once she was in bed, and the lights were off, her mind wouldn't stop racing with thoughts. But there was one thought that ate at her the most: *How am I ever going to afford a lawyer?*

\* \* \*

Mackenzie did her best to get through her day. She had gotten Hope to school, and she had gotten to the bakery early so she could start tackling the special orders that were starting to pile up. It was the first time she had ever wished to be *less* busy at the bakery. She had dozed off a couple of times, but when her eyes popped wide-open at 3:00 a.m., that was it for sleep. For the next two hours, she had stared into the darkness, frustrated and growing increasingly angry as time crept along. And now, thanks to Dylan, her eyes were burning and puffy from lack of sleep and her head was pounding.

"This is the last of them." Mackenzie boxed up the specialty cupcakes she had just frosted. She tiredly stacked the box with the rest of the special orders to be picked up by customers, and then took off her apron.

"Do you mind closing up for me today, Molly?" Mackenzie asked her manager.

"I don't mind a bit, little one. I've got nothin' but dirty laundry and drama waiting for me at home. I come to work to get away from it." Molly belly laughed. "Go home and get some rest. You're working yourself too hard."

Sitting in her car, Mackenzie truly wished she could take that advice. But she couldn't. She had ignored her phone all day in order to get through the special orders. Now she needed to deal with Dylan. He had called and she hadn't trusted herself to answer when she still had orders to fill. When she listened to his message, she was puzzled by the fact that he hadn't mentioned the letter from his attorney. He wanted to know if she was attending the emergency meeting at Pegasus.

"*What* emergency meeting?" she asked herself aloud.

Instead of dialing Dylan's number first, Mackenzie called Aggie.

"Aggie, it's Mackenzie… What's this I hear about an emergency meeting?"

"The owners've sold the property right out from underneath us. Our lease runs out in a month, we've gotten a notice to vacate and we've got no place to go. And even if we *did* have a place to go, we don't have enough money to get there. The grants've dried up, the donations've dried up… I was countin' on our annual fundraiser to pull us through another six months. Now that's off. We're in real trouble here…"

Rayna and Charlie had already agreed to watch Hope after school so she could get caught up at work and deal with Dylan. From Dylan's message, she knew that he intended to attend the meeting at Pegasus. She hadn't planned to confront him in a public venue, but at this point she didn't care. She would see what she could do to help Aggie and then she would find a way to handle her business *discreetly* with Dylan.

By the time she arrived at Pegasus, a record number of volunteers had crammed themselves into the narrow, dusty office. Everyone was tightly packed in the hot space, and the air was already muggy and stale. The volunteers wore worried tense faces as they wiped sweat from their brows and the back of their necks.

Mackenzie wound her way through the crowd to get closer to where Aggie was stationed. At the front of the pack now, Mackenzie spotted Dylan standing to Aggie's right. He was still dressed in business attire, complete with tie, slacks, cuff links and polished wing tips. She didn't imagine it. She knew she didn't imagine it. His eyes had lit up when he saw her and he had smiled at her in greeting. It amazed her how *cavalier* he could be about turning his attorney loose on her.

*Jerk!*

After the initial eye contact, Mackenzie refused to look at him. She kept her eyes aimed directly on Aggie, and did her best to focus on the crisis at hand. She would get to Dylan soon enough.

For a moment, Dylan was distracted by the daggers in Mackenzie's eyes that seemed to be aimed directly at him. And he was really certain that he hadn't done anything wrong. Maybe she was having a rotten day. Maybe she was understandably concerned about the fate of Pegasus. But she had looked at him as if he was enemy number one and now she was refusing to make eye contact with him at all.

*What the heck did I do?*

"The bottom line here is that we've got to relocate the horses and we've got a month to do it. We're gonna have to call all our riders and cancel this month's sessions so we can give this situation our total attention. I hate to do it, but it's got to be done. I need volunteers to start shaking some of our donors' trees to see if anything'll fall out. And I need everyone to start looking for a place where we can stable thirty horses." Aggie's sharp voice ricocheted in the small space. Her face was beet red, her deep-set eyes blazing mad. "If we can't get this done…if we can't find a place for all of 'em, we're not gonna have any choice but to split 'em up. And that'll be the end of Pegasus until we can regroup. That's what we're lookin' at. That's how serious this is."

Murmurs of concern and distress rippled through the group, while Aggie took a moment to collect her emotions. Dylan was standing close enough to her to see that her eyes, for a split second, had teared up.

"So…I appreciate all of you comin' out here today on short notice. All I can say now is let's get to work and make this happen."

Aggie abruptly ended the meeting and went through

the side door that led to the barn. Dylan went directly to Mackenzie's side; he waited patiently for her to finish talking to one of the other volunteers.

"I don't want Hope to know about this." Mackenzie was firm when she said this. "She's got enough to deal with right now."

"That's fine." Dylan took a step closer to her so a volunteer could walk behind him. "Hey…are you mad at me for some reason?"

Mackenzie shook her head in disgust. "You're joking, right?"

Surprised and confused, Dylan glanced around at the crowd and decided that they needed to go somewhere with fewer ears listening.

"Let's go outside," Dylan leaned down and said closer to her ear.

Mackenzie acknowledged everyone she passed, hugging some, commiserating with others, until she found her way out of the humid office and into fresher early-evening air. Dylan was on her heels, keeping pace with her as she made her way back to her car. She unlocked the doors.

"Get in." All of the anger and hurt she had been suppressing during the day was rushing to the surface, making it difficult for her to maintain a civil tone.

Dylan closed the door behind him; he had no idea what had set Mackenzie off like this. He hadn't done anything wrong!

"This week just keeps on getting better and better," Mackenzie muttered. She dug through her bag and pulled out an envelope. She thrust it toward him. "I got your little list of demands, Dylan. You want regular, *scheduled* visitation? You want to legally mandate that you're the only man Hope can call Dad? Are you *insane*? I'm not going to *force* my daughter to call you *Dad* if she doesn't want to do it!"

Astonished and confused, Dylan took the envelope. He pulled out the papers and studied them.

"These weren't supposed to be sent to you yet," he said.

"*Yet*? Why would you send them to me *ever*?" Mackenzie snapped at him. "What made you go behind my back and get an attorney? I've *never* put any pressure on you, I've *never* made any demands! All I asked was that you spend time with her. Get to know her. *Love* her..."

"I do love her." Dylan tucked the papers back into the envelope. "And I'm sorry that you got these papers. It was a mistake and I'll handle it. But the fact is, Mackenzie, you're the one holding all the cards. I wanted to know my rights, so I went to a lawyer. You had to at least suspect that I would..."

"Did you—" Mackenzie stopped talking for a minute to smile and wave at the volunteers walking past the car "—hire this attorney before or after we slept together?"

There was a long pause, a guilty pause, before Dylan admitted, "Before."

"That's just great, Dylan." Mackenzie pulled the envelope out of his hand and stuffed it in her tote. "That's just *great*." Mackenzie leaned back, gripped the steering wheel with her hands. She refused to look at him. "The worst part is that I had actually started to allow myself to care about you. I'd actually let myself start to think that maybe we could give Hope what she's been missing for a long time...a mom *and* a dad."

"We still can..."

Mackenzie bit her lip hard to stop tears from forming. She refused to cry in front of him over this.

"You *slept* with me knowing that you were going to serve me with papers! Why would I ever trust you again after you did a snake-in-the-grass thing like that?"

"You came to my room, Mackenzie. Not the other way around."

"You didn't have to say *yes*."

"I wanted to say yes! You're a beautiful woman. You asked me to make love to you and I *did*. And I don't regret it!"

"I'm sure you don't…"

Dylan looked up at the roof of the car, shook his head and then said, "I'm sorry you got the papers. I am. But I'm *not* going to apologize for going to an attorney so I know my rights. I've tried to talk to you about this before and you've always shut me down. You shut me down all the time, Mackenzie. You know you do."

In response, Mackenzie grabbed her keys off the console and stuck them into the ignition.

"Just forget it, Dylan. We're not going to solve anything tonight. I have a ton to do to get the bakery ready for the weekend, Hope has chemo on Friday, Pegasus is falling apart, and now, thanks to you, I have to figure out how in the world I'm going to get the money for a lawyer. Can this week *get* any better?"

"You don't have to get a lawyer…"

"Oh yes, I do." Mackenzie cranked the engine. "Please get out of my car."

Dylan stood in the empty spot where her Chevy had been parked and watched Mackenzie's taillights disappear around the corner. He'd never in his life seen Mackenzie lose her temper like that. She was understandably furious and he knew he'd screwed up big-time with her. And so, apparently, did everyone else.

"What the hell did you do to Mackenzie?" This was Ian's greeting when he picked up the phone.

"I took your advice and went to see Ben."

Dylan could hear Jordan commenting loudly in the

background. "I didn't tell you to serve her with papers. And now Jordan's walking around all pissed off at me..."

"Mackenzie called Jordan...?"

"Of course she did. And Jordan knows Levine is one of my friends."

"Sorry, man..."

"Don't apologize. Fix it. I don't like it when Jordan's pissed off at me. And now she's determined for us to pay Mackenzie's legal fees."

"Oh...crap..."

"My sentiments exactly. I'm telling you, I do *not* want to be caught up in the middle of this. I love you, you're my best friend, but you need to straighten this crap out right now."

"She wasn't supposed to get the papers, okay? Ben told his paralegal not to file them and she made a mistake and mailed them instead."

"I hope he fired her," Ian snapped.

"What does it matter? The papers were sent. The damage is already done." Dylan rubbed his forehead. "Look... tell Jordan that I'll fix it, okay? But in the meantime, I need a favor..."

There was a long pause and in the background he could still hear Jordan blowing her top. "Can you *hear* what's going on behind me?"

"I hear it..."

"And you're still asking me for a favor?"

"Yes...I know my timing sucks...but, yeah."

Two days after Mackenzie had received the papers, she was still refusing to take his calls. He had intended to give her a couple more days to cool off. But he wasn't going to wait indefinitely. He knew Hope was scheduled to have chemo and he didn't want to be shut out of these critical moments in his daughter's life anymore. And even though he realized that Mackenzie had good reason to be mad at him, he had actually started to think that maybe he had a good reason to be upset with *her*. He wanted to be there for Hope in all the ways that mattered. But as far as the world was concerned, he wasn't her father and he didn't have any rights where she was concerned. That was Mackenzie's doing and he was justified in wanting it to be *un*-done. He had actually worked himself up pretty good, so he sounded less than conciliatory when Mackenzie surprised him with a phone call. If she wanted to start round number two, he was willing.

"Dylan?" There was a distinct waver in her voice. Mackenzie didn't sound mad. She sounded upset, as if she was fighting to hold herself together.

Dylan was on his way to meet Ian at their CPA's office to discuss the tax implications of expanding their business. His fingers flexed on the steering wheel hard when he heard the raw emotion in Mackenzie's voice. She wasn't calling to pick a fight.

"Hold on a minute, Mackenzie. I'm driving. Let me pull over so we can talk."

Dylan pulled into a parking lot, turned off the engine.

"What's wrong?" he asked.

"Hope was admitted into the hospital. She…relapsed." Mackenzie's voice cracked. "She's scheduled to have a lumbar puncture today…she wants to see you, Dylan. Will you come?"

"I'm on my way."

Dylan turned around and headed toward the hospital. He called Ian on the way and canceled their meeting. Never in his life had he felt the way he was feeling now. He had loved people before. He had loved friends, family…women.

Mackenzie. But what he felt for Hope…that was an entirely new type of love.

Dylan worked to look calm on the outside. He wanted to be an anchor for Hope. But on the inside he was panicked. Dylan had been walking quickly right up until he reached the wing that housed Hope's room. He slowed down, even stopped a couple of times, trying to collect himself before he went into her room.

*Pull yourself together, man.*

But it was a hard thing to do. He was scared out of his gourd, and completely out of his league. The antiseptic smell of the hospital made him feel sick to his stomach. The beeping of the blood pressure machines, the buzzing at the nurses' stations, the coldness of the hallways, all unearthed memories that he had tried to keep buried. His mom had died in a place like this. Would his daughter die in a place like this, too?

"Look who's here, Hope." Mackenzie's face was drawn and tight. Her eyes were bloodshot from stress and worry.

Hope looked so small, so fragile, in that hospital bed. She was hooked up to IVs and monitors. Dark circles ringed her dull eyes. Her sweet round face was pale; her freckles contrasted with the sallow coloring of her face. This was not the same girl he'd seen less than a week ago.

"Hey, Hope," Dylan said from the doorway.

Mackenzie pointed to the wall next to the door. "There's hand sanitizer right there."

Dylan sanitized his hands before he pulled a chair up to the side of Hope's bed.

"Are you going to go see Gypsy tomorrow?" Hope's lips were dry, her voice weaker than usual.

"Of course…" Dylan smiled at her. "Of course I am."

"Will you give her a carrot for me? I don't want her to think that I forgot about her."

Dylan swallowed hard several times, pushing his emotions down with each swallow. "I'll get some carrots on the way home tonight."

"But don't give them to her by hand. Put them in her bucket."

Dylan nodded, reached for her hand and squeezed it reassuringly. Hope looked at him in the eyes, and then her face crumpled. Tears streamed down his daughter's face, her eyes shut tightly. Paralyzed, Dylan didn't know what to do.

"I'm going to miss the field trip." Hope hid her face in the thin white hospital blanket that covered her bed. "And I'm going to lose all my hair again."

Hope collapsed into Mackenzie's arms. Above Hope's head, Dylan's and Mackenzie's eyes met. And a silent agreement passed between them. A truce. Their disagreement washed away by Hope's tears. They had to be on the same team. They both had to be on Hope's team.

## Chapter Thirteen

Watching Mackenzie help get Hope ready for the spinal tap gave him a new perspective on the mother of his child. There was a moment when Mackenzie was able to rise above her emotions to help the medical team like a pro. She was calm, collected, a steady hand for their daughter. He was impressed…from a distance. In business meetings, he was usually the guy at the head of the table. The guy with all the answers. But here? He was useless. And it didn't feel good.

Hope was given medication to help her relax. The medication would help her stay motionless during the procedure but would also allow her rest afterward. Mackenzie helped the nurse gently guide Hope onto her side and curled her into the fetal position. Hope wasn't crying anymore; in fact, once the procedure began, she didn't move and she didn't make a sound. Mackenzie ran her hand soothingly over the top of Hope's head. Hope's bare skin was exposed for the nurse to sterilize the area and apply anesthetic cream to her lower spine.

"You're a champ, Hope. Just hang in there and we'll be done before you know it," the doctor said as she prepared to puncture Hope's skin with the long needle.

Dylan caught Mackenzie's eye right before he ducked out of the room. He'd chickened out; he couldn't handle it. He hadn't been prepared, mentally, for this part of Hope's life. Yes, he knew she had been diagnosed with leukemia. Yes, he knew that she had to take daily medicine and weekly medicine, that she had a permanent port just below her collarbone for chemotherapy and blood tests. But knowing about something and *seeing* something were two different things. He had never seen her port before today. And no one in his life had ever needed a spinal tap before.

Thankfully, the entire procedure, from start to finish, took less than forty-five minutes, but to Dylan, it seemed as if he had exiled himself to the hallway for a much longer time. He heard the doctor tell Mackenzie that they should have the results back from the lab in a few hours and then doctor and nurse walked hurriedly out of the room, one right after the other, and on to their next patient. Dylan poked his head into the room; Mackenzie was tucking the blanket tightly around Hope's body. Hope had her eyes closed when her mother kissed her on the forehead. Mackenzie turned off the light to Hope's room, left the door cracked open and joined him in the hall.

"Sorry...I couldn't watch..." Dylan hoped that she didn't think less of him because he had left the room.

"I know...it's hard. I never get used to it."

"It didn't seem that way to me. I didn't even see you flinch."

"Oh, well...I've learned how to fake stability." Mackenzie smiled weakly. "But don't be fooled. My legs shake every time."

"Every time? Has she had a lot of these?" Dylan asked, surprised.

Mackenzie nodded. "That's how they check to make sure that the cells haven't spread to the spinal fluid. All we can do now is pray that they haven't."

They fell silent, two pensive figures motionless in the midst of the bustling backdrop of the hospital. It wasn't fair, to be standing here with Mackenzie. Hope should be in school and looking forward to riding Gypsy. She shouldn't be in a hospital bed, preparing for an intense round of treatment.

"Have you eaten?" It was the only thing he could think to ask at the moment.

"Uh-uh. No. I haven't had a chance. But I don't want to leave in case Hope needs me."

"I'll stay with her. You've got to eat."

"Are you sure?"

"I want to help you." Dylan wasn't used to feeling as if he didn't have something important to contribute to a situation.

A break would be nice actually. She had skipped breakfast and her stomach was so empty that it hurt. And there were phone calls that still needed to be made. Hope could be in the hospital for a while so this was her new temporary home. Arrangements had to be made. She'd have to contact the school, maybe bring in extra help at the bakery so they didn't fall behind. There was so much to do.

Mackenzie quickly grabbed her phone and wallet out of her tote. "Just make sure that she stays on her back, okay? I won't be long."

"Mackenzie…" Dylan saying her name made her stop.

She turned, took a step toward him, and he took a step toward her.

"I wanted to say…" He started to apologize, but the expression on her face stopped him.

"Can we just…not…right now?" Mackenzie asked him. She was exhausted, and stressed, and even though she was hiding it well, he knew that she was terrified that the cancer had come back. If she wanted to table the apology, he would table the apology. No questions asked.

"Sure…" Dylan had to put his hands in his pockets to stop himself from reaching out to her. She looked as if she desperately needed a hug; he wanted to comfort her. Was she receptive to that kind of support from him? He doubted it.

"Take your time." Dylan watched her walk down the hall. Mackenzie turned her head to look back at him, saw him standing there and smiled fleetingly before she disappeared around the corner.

Dylan closed the door behind him to keep the bright hallway light from flooding into the room. Sitting next to her bed, he marveled at the fact that anyone managed to rest in a place that made so much noise. Doctors being paged, nurses checking on patients, carts rolling loudly by. And if the noise didn't disturb you, the regular "vital signs" visits would. That's what eventually awakened his daughter. After a chubby nurse's assistant with a Minnie Mouse voice took Hope's vital signs, she looked up at him groggily, her eyes barely open.

"Where's Mom?" she asked. Her voice was weak, her lips very dry.

Dylan poured her a glass of water from the pitcher, took the straw out of the wrapper and dropped it into the disposable cup.

"She went to go get something to eat. She'll be back

soon. Here…" Dylan held the straw up to Hope's lips. Hope took a couple of small sips and then turned her head away to signal that she'd had enough.

Dylan put the cup down on the rolling table and sat down in the chair. Hope's eyes were closed again; he thought, for a moment, that she had drifted back to sleep. He reached through the metal bed rails so he could slip his palm under hers. Hope squeezed his fingers.

"Dad?" Hope's voice was so quiet and raspy that Dylan wasn't sure he'd heard her right. Had she just called him Dad for the first time?

"Dad?" Hope said again, this time more loudly…more distinctly.

"I'm right here, Hope…" Dylan couldn't have predicted what hearing that one word would make him feel. He knew he was Hope's father, but this was the first time that he truly felt like her dad.

"I'm cold."

Finally, something he *could* fix. Dylan flagged down a passing nurse and requested extra blankets. Dylan hovered by the door until the heated blankets arrived. Dylan quickly covered her with the blankets. He tucked the edges tightly around Hope the way he had seen Mackenzie do for her.

"Better?" he asked.

Hope nodded her response, never opening her eyes.

A few minutes later, Mackenzie came through the door.

"Everything okay?" she whispered from Hope's bedside.

Dylan gave one quiet nod. He almost told her about what had just happened. He almost did. But then he thought better of it. Mackenzie might not be so excited about the news and she had enough on her plate right now to deal with.

Dylan stood up so Mackenzie could take the most comfortable chair closest to the bed. He checked his watch. They still had another couple of hours before they would hear the results of the lumbar puncture. He picked up the chair by the door, moved it closer to the bed, sat down and started to scroll through his emails on his phone. Now he knew to bring his computer. In between reading and answering email, Dylan would look up from the task and watch his daughter sleep. Before today, he'd never tucked her into bed. Before today, she had always called him Dylan.

*Dad*, Dylan thought in amazement. *I'm Dad*.

Two weeks into Hope's hospital stay, Dylan started to feel like a seasoned hospital patron. He knew where he could find good hot coffee at just about any hour of the day or night. He knew when to eat at the cafeteria and when to avoid it like the plague. He knew the nurses, and custodians, and volunteers by name. And, unfortunately, he now knew more about steroids, and chemotherapy, and flushing ports than he had ever *wanted* to know. It was gut-wrenching to watch when Hope was at her worst. And, because of the relapse, the treatment protocol was much more aggressive. But the leukemia cells hadn't reached the spinal cord and that gave them reason to believe that a second remission could be on the horizon.

"I thought I'd find you out here." Mackenzie was wise to his best hiding spots. Sometimes he just needed to get away. Sometimes he just needed to *escape* the reality of the hospital.

Dylan scooted over so she could join him on the wrought-iron bench. This small, secluded courtyard was his favorite of his hiding spots. He'd eaten a lot of bag lunches under the shade of this old blue oak tree.

Mackenzie's hair was pulled back in a loose ponytail

and she was wearing the same Padres jersey she had worn the night they had kissed for the first time. There were so many times over these last weeks that Dylan craved Mackenzie. He wanted that physical connection with her. He wanted to love her and *be* loved by her, particularly during some of the worst moments with Hope. But she always kept him just an arm's length away. Close, but not *too* close.

Dylan reached inside his computer bag and pulled out a stack of her medical bills. He had come to her a week ago and insisted that she let him help her with the expenses. In the end, she couldn't argue with his logic. The stress of unpaid medical bills hanging over her head and ruining her credit was only funneling her vital energy away from Hope.

"These are paid."

Mackenzie stared at the large stack of envelopes on the bench between them. These envelopes had dogged her for years. They had robbed her of sleep; they had caused her so much stress and worry. And then, just like that…with no real fanfare, they were gone.

"Thank you…" Mackenzie reached for them. "Thank you."

"Thank you for letting me help." Dylan closed the lid of his laptop. "Is she still working with the tutor?"

She nodded yes. Hope was an overachieving kind of student, which she came by honestly from her mom. Other than her hair falling out again, the two things that really upset Hope about the relapse were missing school and missing out on Pegasus.

"Any updates from Aggie?" Mackenzie hated that she couldn't be more involved with solving Pegasus's crisis. As long as Hope was in the hospital, everything had to be put on hold. Even Pegasus.

"I think we've nailed down a viable option."

"Are you serious?"

When Dylan confirmed what he had just said, Mackenzie closed her eyes, her face tilted upward for a moment.

"Oh, thank goodness…" Now she could break *good* news to Hope instead of heartbreaking news.

"Where in the world did Aggie find a place that could take that many horses on short notice?"

When Dylan wasn't with Hope, he spent his wait time at the hospital trying to run down leads to place the horses. But what they really needed was more time, more money and a miracle.

"We're moving them out to Aunt Gerri's," Dylan said.

Mackenzie stared at him, shocked into silence. After a second or two, she asked, "Aunt Gerri is donating the farm to *Pegasus*?"

Dylan shook his head. "No. I would never ask her to do that. That's her retirement."

Dylan answered the question in Mackenzie's eyes.

"We're going to buy it from her."

"Pegasus is going to buy your aunt's farm? How? That land has to be worth…*millions*."

"It is…"

"They can't afford that! I've seen Aggie struggle to buy enough hay some months…."

Dylan rubbed the stubble on his chin and face. The stress in Mackenzie's voice matched the stress that he had been feeling for weeks. He had no real idea how to make the farm work in the long term for Pegasus; all he had was a short-term plan. He was the numbers guy and the numbers just didn't work. Not yet.

"My aunt's agreed to let us lease the land for now." Getting his kindhearted aunt to agree to lend a hand had been the easy part. It was the logistics of the move that were the problem. Yes, they had plenty of volunteers willing to help and they had enough trailers lined up to accommodate the horses. But the farm hadn't housed horses for years. The infrastructure had deteriorated, the two standing barns needed to be cleaned out and cleaned up. The fences needed to be mended so they could use the pastures. And all of that took money. They'd already raised a decent chunk of change, but they needed more to buy the land. Lots of it.

"And…" Dylan continued. "We've already raised right around two hundred thousand dollars, so we've got some capital to work with…"

"Wait a minute…did you just say…two hundred *thousand*?" When Dylan confirmed the number, Mackenzie said, "You did this…"

It was a statement, not a question.

Dylan stood up and held out his hand to her. "I really need something to drink. Walk with me?"

She put her hand into his but her eyes never left his face. This man had grown; he had matured. In just a short few months, he had begun to care more about the condition of the world around him. And he had been a tireless support these last weeks at the hospital. Everyone had noticed it: Rayna, Charlie…Jordan.

"How did you pull this off, Dylan?" Dry, brittle leaves crunched beneath their feet as they walked slowly across the courtyard.

"Trust me…I couldn't do that on my own. I'm just good at turning money into more money, not fundraising. Some of the money came from our regular donors, Ian's been contacting some of our previous clients looking for sponsors, and I think your cousin, Josephine, is it? Her boyfriend's parents have some pretty deep pockets…"

Mackenzie walked through the door Dylan held open for her. "How much did you donate?"

Dylan followed her through the door. "I donated some."

"How much?"

"Some…"

Mackenzie stopped walking. "Dylan…how much of that two hundred thousand came from you?"

Dylan sighed, stopped walking and made a small U-turn so he could stand directly in front of her.

"How much?" Her eyebrows lifted with the question.

Dylan glanced around before he said, "A hundred…"

"Dollars?"

"No…" Dylan lowered his voice. "Thousand…"

Mackenzie was dumbstruck. She studied Dylan's tired eyes and then it clicked in her brain.

"You sold your Corvette…" She said that and Dylan stopped meeting her gaze. "Oh, Dylan…you didn't…"

Dylan turned his head away from her. "Don't make a big deal out of it, Mackenzie."

"Don't make a big *deal* out of it? That car meant *everything* to you."

"No. It didn't." Dylan's eyes were back on her. "Hope means everything to me. Okay? *You* mean everything to me."

Mackenzie swallowed hard several times to keep her emotions in check. She refused to let herself cry in the middle of the hospital lobby. But she wanted to cry. Eyes watery with emotion, Mackenzie asked Dylan, "Can I hug you?"

The pain in his eyes when she asked that question made her feel like a genuine jerk. She knew that Dylan had wanted to be consoled by her for weeks. She knew it. And yet, she hadn't done the one thing for this man that he needed from her. It was such a simple thing and she had denied him.

Dylan didn't nod, he didn't say yes; he opened his arms to her instead. She was the one to close the distance between them. He had already taken nine figurative steps toward her over the past few months, and it was her turn finally to take that one *literal* step toward him. They embraced, right there in the middle of the busy hospital lobby. Dylan held on to her so tightly. And she held on to him. When they were face-to-face, body to body, arms intertwined, Mackenzie could feel that they were a perfect fit. A perfect match. Hugging Dylan…being hugged by Dylan… was the most comfortable, reassuring experience she could remember having. Everything but Dylan, and the feel of his body, faded far into the background.

"Thank you…" Mackenzie rested her head on his shoulder.

Dylan's arms tightened around her, she felt him kiss the top of her head. "I've missed you."

Mackenzie leaned back a bit so she could put her hand on Dylan's face. "You're such a good man, Dylan Axel."

Dylan reached up and captured her hand, pressed his lips to her palm and then held her hand next to his heart. "I've always wanted you to think so. Even when we were kids."

"I do think so…what you've done for Hope…what you've done for me." Even though she had called a truce with him that first day in the hospital, this was the moment when she was truly able to release her resentment over the attorney's letter.

Dylan took a chance. The way she was looking at him, he wanted to believe that there was an invitation in her eyes. He kissed her. Gently, sweetly, tenderly.

"People are staring…" Mackenzie said when the kiss ended.

Dylan glanced around for a second then grabbed her hand. Instead of heading toward the cafeteria, Dylan started walking back toward the courtyard. He led her through the door, across the courtyard and behind the large blue oak tree. Hidden behind the thick trunk of the tree, Dylan pulled Mackenzie back into his arms and kissed her. The first kiss had been a question. The second kiss was a lover's demand. He leaned back against the tree and brought her with him. He deepened the kiss, teasing her tongue with his.

Ultimately, it was Dylan who ended the kisses. He held her by the shoulders, pinning her with narrowed, intense eyes. "I have to stop."

Mackenzie agreed. They needed to stop. If only it hadn't felt so good. If only she didn't want to kiss him again… right now.

"You've never let me apologize for not telling you that I had gone to an attorney. I've tried…more than once."

"I know…" He had tried, but just as he had said to her during their disagreement at Pegasus, she always changed the subject.

"Do you forgive me, Mackenzie? Can we move on now?"

"I forgive you," she said, and meant it.

Mackenzie's phone chimed; she checked it.

"Hope's done with tutoring," she said. "I need to get back to her. Can we…talk more later?"

Dylan nodded his agreement.

"Are you coming?" Mackenzie paused when he didn't follow her.

"In a minute…" Dylan glanced down toward the bulge near his zipper.

She wasn't really a blusher, but she did then. "Oh…do you want me to wait, too?"

"No. You go ahead. I'll catch up in a minute." While he was waiting, he realized how much his reality had shifted since Mackenzie and Hope. A couple of months ago, he was a successful business owner with a lot of time for parties, surfing and hot blondes. Now? He hadn't thrown a party since Ian's birthday, he had become a philanthropist, a curvy brunette had replaced the blonde and the Corvette was gone.

But that was all superficial stuff and now he knew it. The biggest change was the change that had happened in his heart. He discovered that he liked having a daughter. He liked being a dad and he was pretty good at it so far. In fact, he had started to think that he'd like to have more children. This time he'd be there from conception to birth and beyond. And he wanted to have those children with Mackenzie. She was the one for him. He loved her and when the moment was right, he was going to propose marriage. She might not know it yet, but Dylan was determined to marry Mackenzie.

## *Chapter Fourteen*

One week at the hospital could feel like a month. Dylan had passed exhaustion a while ago and was now operating in a zone teetering somewhere between comatose and hysteria. He had taken to sleeping on his favorite courtyard bench and didn't even care anymore that he must look like a homeless person sleeping off a bender. Mackenzie rarely left the hospital, and when she did leave, it was to get something done for the bakery or go to Hope's school for a meeting. She hadn't had a real break, or real sleep, in weeks. And they were both starting to fray around the edges. The littlest thing would make them snap at each other, and there was a bite in their tone that was a symptom of their extreme fatigue and chronic worry. Mackenzie had let Rayna or Charlie stay with Hope during the day, but she had refused to leave Hope overnight. Mackenzie needed to get some actual sleep in an actual bed, and he was going to force the issue today.

"Uh…*wow*! You look like total crap!" Jordan met up with him at the hospital entrance, carrying her motorcycle helmet under her arm.

He could tell by the look on her fact that Jordan was shocked by his appearance. He couldn't really blame her; he was usually the stylish guy in the group. Even on casual days, Dylan wore slacks, button-down shirts, his customary Rolex watch and expensive shoes. Today, he was in a T-shirt, jeans and sneakers. His hair was shaggy, as if he'd missed his bimonthly appointment with the barber, and she had never seen him with a five-o'clock shadow before.

"Thanks for coming." Dylan hugged Jordan, glad to see her.

"Of course. What else?" Jordan asked. "Is Mackenzie really going to let me take a shift? I've been offering for weeks."

Dylan opened the door for her. "I'm not going to give her a choice. If I have to, I'll throw her over my shoulder and carry her out of here."

"Well, all right, caveman." Jordan laughed at the thought. "That'll go over well. If I were you, when you put her down, run like hell. Mackenzie may be little, but she packs a punch."

"Trust me—" Dylan pushed the button for the elevator "—I know."

Just outside Hope's room, Dylan slipped on a paper hospital mask. "Wait here for a minute, okay?"

Jordan waited for Dylan while he went into the room. The room was dimly lit because Hope was resting. Mackenzie was doing her best to sleep curled up in the chair. He had tried to sleep in that chair himself, so he knew how uncomfortable it was. He knelt down beside Mackenzie and rested his hand on her thigh.

"Mackenzie…" he whispered.

"Hmm?" Mackenzie cracked her eyes open.

"Come outside with me for a minute…"

"Why?"

"Just come outside with me…"

Mackenzie pushed herself upright slowly, yawned behind her mask and rubbed her eyes. Finally, she stood up, stretched her arms above her head and followed him quietly out of the room.

Mackenzie slipped off her mask. "Jordan!"

The cousins hugged each other in greeting.

"I wish you'd let me know you were coming. Hope's asleep. She's going to be really upset that she missed you."

"She's not gonna miss me," Jordan said. "I'm spending the night."

Mackenzie looked between Dylan and her cousin. "You are?"

"You need to sleep in your own bed, Mackenzie. You haven't slept in weeks." Dylan put his hand on her shoulder.

"No…" Mackenzie shook her head. To Jordan she said, "Thank you, but no."

Jordan was a good match for Mackenzie. They didn't resemble each other, but they were cut from the same tough cloth. Jordan had a really good chance of winning this round.

"You're welcome, and *yes*. You're going home. I'm staying here," Jordan said in a no-nonsense tone. "Hope's my family. You're my family. I get to help."

Mackenzie wasn't a shrinking violet, but she was a *weary* violet. "All right."

Dylan was surprised at how quickly Mackenzie gave in to her cousin, but he wasn't about to wait around to let her change her mind. He hustled her back into the room to grab her tote and kiss a still-sleeping Hope goodbye. He handed Jordan a mask.

"You have to wear this all the time. No fruit, no flowers. I'm going to drive Mackenzie home. Call *me*, not her, if you need something."

"No…she needs to call me…" Mackenzie disagreed. Over her shoulder, she said to Jordan, "You need to call me."

"*Go*…both of you." Jordan had her mask on. "I've got this."

Jordan watched her cousin and Dylan walk away together. Mackenzie had her arm linked with his and Dylan had the look of a man in love. Dylan and Mackenzie? On paper, they seemed like a really odd match, but, when Jordan saw them together, they just *fit*. Sometimes opposites really did attract.

Dylan drove Mackenzie home in his car, leaving her car parked at the hospital. She twisted to the side in the bucket seat, facing him, and closed her eyes. He typed her address into the GPS. He knew that she lived near Balboa Park, but he'd never been to her house.

Mackenzie wasn't asleep on the way home; she was just too tired to keep her eyes open. She was so exhausted that she felt sick with it. When Jordan showed up, she knew that Dylan had arranged it and that he was right. It was time for her to get some rest. If she got sick, then she wouldn't even be able to go into Hope's room, much less stay with her overnight.

Mackenzie heard the robotic voice of the GPS say the name of her street. She sat up, yawned loudly and then pointed to her small Spanish-style bungalow.

"That's me right there on the left."

Dylan pulled up in front of her house and parked. He

walked quickly to her side of the car, opened the door and held out his hand to her.

"Nice place." Dylan walked beside her up to the front door.

"Thank you. Hope and I love it here." Mackenzie turned off the alarm remotely and then slipped the key into the door. "Do you want to come in?"

"Sure…" He had been hoping for an invitation but wasn't so sure he'd get one.

Mackenzie walked in first, and then stepped to the side so he could come in. "You may as well see what you're getting yourself into…"

The way Mackenzie had described her penchant for messiness, he had been worried about what he may find behind the door. He was relieved to find that the quaint, shabby-chic bungalow was a little cluttered—a little disorganized. But it was clean. He could work with that.

Mackenzie dropped her tote and keys on the kitchen counter. "I have to sit down for a minute."

Dylan looked at her small curio cabinet tucked in the corner. "What's this?"

"I collect hearts," Mackenzie said with a yawn. "My mom had a heart collection and I just kept it going. Do you want to sit down?"

She put all the recipe boxes off the love seat onto the floor so Dylan would have a spot to sit. He joined her on the love seat; they sat shoulder to shoulder, thigh to thigh in the quiet living room.

Mackenzie sighed. "This is what I'm going to do… I'm going to take a really hot shower and then get into bed."

"Sounds like a plan," Dylan agreed.

Mackenzie turned her head toward him. "You can either go home, or you can join me. It's up to you."

Her words were blunt, to the point and completely unexpected. But his decision was an easy one to make.

"I want to stay with you..."

Mackenzie stood under the steaming hot water for a long time, letting the heat beat down on her aching neck and back. Sleeping in a chair had taken its toll on her body. After the shower, she got Dylan a fresh towel and one of Hope's unopened One Direction toothbrushes from under the sink. Dylan showered, brushed his teeth and shaved his face with a razor Mackenzie had told him was dull from her shaving her legs. He didn't put his clothes back on; instead, he just wrapped the towel around his waist. It wasn't like Mackenzie hadn't seen the goods before.

He carried his clothes down the hall and found Mackenzie already in bed. "Can I throw these into the washing machine?"

Mackenzie had been dozing off. She nodded sleepily. "Behind the sliding doors right behind you. Detergent's on the shelf."

Dylan threw his socks, underwear and T-shirt in the washing machine. He had noticed that Mackenzie had left one side of her small bed open for him, and he was looking forward to occupying it. He'd been thinking about getting Mackenzie back into his arms for the longest time. And tonight...*finally*...was the night. Dylan dropped his towel by the side of the bed; if Mackenzie minded that he was getting into her bed in the buff, she didn't say. She watched him, eyes half-mast, while he got into her bed. He was the first man she'd ever had in this bed, and she was glad that she had invited him to stay.

"Do you want me to hold you?" Dylan asked.

Mackenzie turned over and scooted back into his awaiting arms. Dylan wrapped his arm around her body, buried his face in her sweet-smelling neck and closed his eyes.

It didn't take but a minute for his body to start getting worked up over having her in his arms. She was warm and soft and sexy, and even as tired as he was, his body still wanted to make love. Knowing how sleep deprived Mackenzie was, Dylan moved his hips back slightly away from Mackenzie's body. She needed sleep, and as much as he wanted to love her right now, he needed to let her rest.

"Good night," she murmured.

When she snuggled even more deeply into his arms, Dylan closed his eyes and sighed contentedly. Relaxed and at home lying next to her, Dylan fell asleep with the certain knowledge that wherever Mackenzie was, that's where he belonged. They slept for hours. It had been dusk when they arrived home, but it was late in the night when Mackenzie awakened. She heard Dylan snoring beside her in the narrow bed, and she could see in the faintly lit room that he had pushed all the covers over onto her side. Not wanting to wake him, Mackenzie carefully peeled the covers back and tried to get off the end of the bed without wiggling the mattress too much.

"Where're you going?" Dylan asked in the dark.

"Bathroom…" Mackenzie whispered.

She slipped into the bathroom, peed, rinsed out her mouth and then opened the door. The light to the bathroom was still on, so Mackenzie got a full-frontal view of a naked Dylan scratching his chest hair just outside the bathroom door. Dylan had been asleep, but the lower half of his body was wide awake.

"I'll meet you back there…" Dylan let out a long yawn before he changed places with her.

Mackenzie hid a smile as she hurried back to bed. She checked her phone. Jordan had sent her a text saying that Hope was doing well. It was 3:00 a.m., which meant she still had some more sleeping to do.

Dylan took care of business in the bathroom, dropped his clothes in the dryer and then came back to bed. He immediately pulled Mackenzie back into his arms. But this time, instead of letting her go back to sleep, he started to drop small butterfly kisses along the back of her neck.

"Mackenzie…" Dylan breathed in her scent.

"Hmm?"

"Do you know that I love you?"

Her eyes had been closed, but she opened them. She turned her head toward the sound of his voice. "No…"

His lips were next to her ear, the feel of his breath sending wonderful chills down her back. Mackenzie shifted her body so she was facing him in the dark.

"Do you know that I'm in love with you?" he asked.

"No." Mackenzie didn't flinch when Dylan's hand slipped under her T-shirt. He slid his hand behind her back and pulled her closer to him.

Dylan found her lips in the dark. Kissed her, long and slow.

"I do love you…" Dylan touched her face, his fingertips tracing the outline of the lips he had just kissed.

"Do you love me, Mackenzie?"

She gently bit the tip of his finger. Her body was already responding to his kisses, to the feel of his lean, muscular body next to hers.

"Yes…" she admitted to him, and to herself.

Over the past several weeks, her feelings had grown for Dylan. They had deepened. When she looked at him, her heart felt full. When he was gone, she missed him. Lately, she had caught herself waiting for his phone calls and texts, and staring at the hospital doorway, awaiting his return. The love that she now knew she felt for Dylan was different than the love she had for Hope, but it was just as strong. She was in love, for the very first time in her life.

"Thank God," he said before he kissed her again. He gathered her into his arms, holding her so tightly as he deepened the kiss.

Without words spoken between them, Dylan stripped off her shirt and panties. His mouth was on one breast, his hand massaging the other. He sucked on her nipple, drawing it into his mouth, teasing it with his tongue, until she couldn't stay quiet. She pressed his head tighter to her breast and moaned softly. She slipped her hand down between their bodies and wrapped her fingers around his long, hard shaft. He groaned and she smiled a lover's smile. Mackenzie pushed on his shoulder so he would lie down on his back.

"What are you doing?" he asked in the dark.

Intent on her mission, she ignored him. He would know her intentions soon enough. His shaft was thick and silky and warm; it felt so good in her hand. The head of his shaft was large, and tasted salty when she drew it into her mouth.

Dylan's next groan was even louder. His fingers were in her hair, his leg muscles tensed in anticipation; Mackenzie was emboldened. Right then and there, he was at her mercy, she was totally in control, while she loved him with her mouth.

"Mackenzie…I don't want you to stop…" Dylan's voice was strained. "But you've got to stop."

Dylan pulled her up on top of him, kissed her and then pushed her onto her back. He was down between her thighs before she could stop him. She hadn't let him do that when they had made love before; this part of lovemaking always embarrassed her. She could give, but it was harder for her to receive.

But the minute she felt his hot mouth on her flesh, she couldn't remember why she'd ever said no to him before. Dylan slid his hands beneath her hips, lifted her body up and loved her with his tongue until she was squirming and aching and crying out for him to put her out of her misery.

Like a stalking tiger, Dylan moved up her body until they were chest to chest. His shaft was pressed into her stomach; she needed it to be pressed inside of her.

"Where are your condoms?" Dylan's teeth grazed her shoulder.

"I don't have any..."

The moment she said those words, it occurred to her that he was asking because *he* didn't have a condom. Dylan's body became very still on top of her.

"You don't have one?" he asked, frustrated.

Mackenzie shook her head. "No."

Dylan dropped his head into her neck, tempted just to lift his hips and slide himself into her tight, wet, warm body, damn the consequences. After a moment of silent debating, Dylan rolled off her body and sat up on the edge of the bed. He hadn't had sex for a month and he'd been too stressed out to worry about masturbating. But now? His body *knew* it had been deprived and it wanted relief ASAP. He was so hard it felt as if the skin was going to split wide open. And even the thought of risking getting Mackenzie pregnant didn't soften it one bit. In fact, the thought of impregnating her again actually turned him on even more.

Cold without his body on top of her, Mackenzie pulled the blankets up over her body. She wanted to scream. Her body was so sexually charged that all she could think about was getting Dylan inside of her. She curled her legs up and tried to stop focusing on the throbbing he had started between her legs. Head in her pillow, she closed her eyes. She opened them when she felt Dylan lift the blanket.

He was on top of her again and he was still aroused;

the head of his shaft was poised just outside the opening of her body. He took her face between his hands.

"Mackenzie?"

A small stream of moonlight had wound its way through the window slats; she could see the strong planes of his face. More important, she could make out his eyes.

"Yes, Dylan?"

"I want you to be my wife. I want to have more children with you."

Mackenzie swallowed hard before she spoke. "Are you asking me to marry you?"

"Yes, I am." He hadn't expected to propose to her tonight. But the moment felt right. "Marry me, Mackenzie."

"Okay…" she said simply.

Dylan reached between their bodies and guided himself in. He slowly, carefully, slid deeper and deeper until he was as deep inside of her as he could be. He waited for her to protest, to be the voice of reason when they both knew the risk. But she didn't. He pulled back, teasing her with sensual, controlled strokes. Her frustrated sounds signaled that she wanted more from him. She wanted more passion, more intensity, more, more, more… So he stopped worrying and gave himself permission just to experience Mackenzie. He deliberately and methodically loved her longer, and with more passion, than he had ever loved anyone before. When he loved her slowly, she demanded that he go faster. When he gave her one orgasm, she pleaded for another. But it was her unbridled, uncensored cry at the peak of her second orgasm that destroyed his carefully manufactured control.

"I'm going to come…do you want me to pull out?" Dylan gritted the words out.

Mackenzie locked her legs around him and kept him right where he was. That simple gesture drove him crazy;

he braced himself above her, arms locked, head thrown back as he exploded inside of her.

Dylan didn't move; he dropped his head down and caught his breath. Then he lowered himself down on top of her.

"Holy Toledo, woman…" Dylan laughed into her neck.

Mackenzie hugged him and laughed, too. She felt satisfied and *sexy*. She didn't even bother to cover her body when Dylan rolled to the side. They both lay on their backs, holding hands, savoring the aftermath of their lovemaking. Each time with Dylan was just a little bit better than the last. She was more comfortable with her own body. She was more comfortable with him. He thought she was beautiful, and she'd only seen him date really gorgeous women. It had helped her to start owning the idea that she was an attractive, curvy woman.

"Do you think that I got you pregnant?" Dylan's question interrupted her own internal dialogue.

Her hand moved down to her abdomen. The timing in her cycle could be right. "I don't know. Maybe."

"And if I did?"

The thought of carrying Dylan's child filled her with an immediate rush of joy. She *wanted* to be pregnant with his child again.

"Then Hope won't be an only child anymore."

He squeezed her fingers. "Will you be happy?"

"Yes…" she reassured him. "I've always wanted another child."

Dylan lifted her hand and kissed it.

"What about you?" she asked. "Will you be happy?"

He propped himself up on his side, put his hand on top of hers. Now they both had their hands on her abdomen.

"I hope I did get you pregnant."

His words were the exact reassurance she needed. She

was the mother of Dylan's child, and now she was going to be his wife. That hadn't always been her dream, but it was now. Still tired from weeks at the hospital, they pulled the covers over their bodies and knew that they should try to get some rest. For now, they had had a temporary reprieve from the harsh reality of hospital life. Dylan held on to her tightly; the warmth of his hairy chest felt so good against her back. He brushed her hair back off her shoulder, tightened his arm around her and let his head sink down into the pillow. He was a father and soon he would be a husband. And, maybe, just maybe, their lovemaking had created a new life tonight. If they hadn't succeeded this time, Dylan was hopeful that Mackenzie would agree to keep on trying until they *did*.

## Chapter Fifteen

Dylan's days of wearing expensive clothes and nice shoes were temporarily on hold. Until Pegasus was moved to the farm, he was relegated to jeans, T-shirts, work boots and a baseball cap. His partner, Ian, was taking charge of the business expansion while he split his time between the hospital and the farm. The new owners of the land Pegasus was currently occupying, investors with a plan to develop, had given them a two-week extension to vacate. It didn't seem like much, but it was actually a donation of sorts. As far as the investors were concerned, every day they delayed their project cost them money. The extra two weeks helped, but there was still a long list of things that needed to be done at the farm in order to keep the horses comfortable. As far as getting Pegasus operational again for riders, that was an entirely different problem for a different day.

He had found his uncle's old tool belt in the shed, and

wearing it made him feel like maybe Bill was watching, guiding him with his steady hand. He was actually surprised at how quickly he had fallen back into life at the farm. He'd even crashed a couple of times in his old room instead of driving back to his place.

"The delivery guy just called!" Doug Silvernail shouted to him from the far end of the barn. "You want them to stack the lumber out front?"

Doug was a contractor at his aunt's church who had donated his time to Pegasus.

"That works, Doug. Thanks!" Dylan shouted back. He pulled off his ball cap, wiped the sweat off his brow and then put the hat back on. He stuffed the sweaty rag back into his pocket and got back to the business of fixing the broken hinge on the stall door. When his phone rang again, which it had been doing nonstop all morning, Dylan cursed under his breath and pulled the phone out of his front pocket.

It was Mackenzie this time. He picked up the call immediately.

"Hey, sweetheart…" He smiled. Talking to Mackenzie was always the best part of his day. Because of his work on behalf of Pegasus, they hadn't been able to spend much time together, but they were in constant contact by phone.

"Dylan…?" The sound of her voice was different. She sounded emotional, and elated. "We just got the test results back…"

Dylan rested his hand on the stall door so all his attention could hone in on Mackenzie's next words.

"She's in remission!"

Relieved, Dylan squeezed his eyes closed for a moment and then looked heavenward. "Oh, thank God!"

He straightened back up, looked upward in gratitude

before he shouted out to the people scattered around the barn. "Hope's in remission! Hope's in remission!"

The people in the barn erupted in cheers. He needed to tell Aunt Gerri right away. On his way out of the barn, some of the volunteers slapped him on the back, shook his hand…it was a day they had all been praying for.

"When can she come home?" Dylan stepped out from the shade of the barn into the bright, hot California sun.

"Tomorrow…" Mackenzie was understandably emotional. He wished he were there to hug her. He wished he could hug both of his girls. "Here…Hope wants to talk to her dad."

Dylan stopped in his tracks. Mackenzie had never called him that before, and she had said it so casually, as if it was no big deal. Hope only called him Dad when Mackenzie wasn't around, so he'd thought that Mackenzie didn't know about it yet. Dylan knew that the subject would have to be broached at some point, but the right moment hadn't presented itself. And, for him, it wasn't urgent. He was going to marry Mackenzie and he was Hope's natural father. That's what mattered. The rest of the stuff would work out eventually.

While he was celebrating with Hope on the phone, Dylan continued on his way to the house. He found his aunt in the kitchen, surrounded by ingredients and pots and pans.

"Hold on, Hope…Aunt Gerri wants to talk to you…" Dylan held the phone out to his aunt. "She's in remission."

Aunt Gerri's face lit up and she tossed up her hands in the air in excitement.

Dylan sat down at the kitchen counter while his aunt chattered excitedly with his daughter. The two of them seemed never to run out of things to say.

"Well, I'm just as happy as I can be, honey…I can't wait to see you. I love you, too," his aunt said before she hung up the phone.

She came around to Dylan's side of the counter and hugged him. "I can't wait until church Wednesday night. The whole congregation's been praying for her!"

His aunt had been in rare form ever since the revolving door of volunteers had started to come to the farm. Her solitary life had vanished and she was thriving. She was energetic and talkative and her kitchen was always open for business. Dylan covered the expense of feeding the volunteer crew, and Gerri was happy to have a reason to cook every day. She fed them and then she played the organ for them. She had been intending to move to town so she could be around people, but for now, the people had come to her.

"Okay…you go do what you know how to do so I can keep doin' what I know how to do. I'll ring the bell when lunch is ready." Gerri had reinstated the practice of ringing the dinner bell Uncle Bill had installed at the back kitchen door.

Dylan opened the back door, but he paused. "Aunt Gerri…?"

"Yes, honey?" Gerri was back to peeling potatoes.

"I'd like to marry Mackenzie here, on the farm. If she likes the idea, would you be okay with it?"

"Well, of course it's okay…this is your home."

It had been a nearly impossible task, but they had managed to pull it off. The two standing barns on the property had been brought back to life. They weren't pretty or perfect, but they were functional for the horses and that's all that mattered at the moment. Uncle Bill had an office space in the main barn, so that's where Aggie would store all of her Pegasus papers, forms and files. The fence around one of the larger pastures had been repaired; some of the horses couldn't be out together; they'd have to rotate the horses until the other fences were fixed. There were still some plumbing issues at both barns, so it was portable restrooms for now. If Dylan thought about all the things left to do, it would drive him nuts. Instead, he tried to concentrate on all the things they had already accomplished.

Even now, riding in the passenger seat of Aggie's truck as she turned up the driveway to the farm, it was still hard for him to believe that this long-anticipated day had finally arrived. He could see Mackenzie and Hope sitting on the porch swing waiting for the horses to arrive at their new home. His aunt appeared from inside the house as the large caravan of trucks, horse trailers, cars filled with volunteers and several rented moving trucks.

"My Bill would be so proud of this day…" Aunt Gerri beamed at Mackenzie and Hope.

Mackenzie put her arm around Gerri's shoulder, and they stood arm and arm, watching the procession head up the winding driveway.

Hope, whose hair had already started to fall out at the hospital, was wearing a bright purple bandanna on her head. Her eyebrows and eyelashes were gone. And she was still pale, thinner than before and still weak from the chemo. There were dark rings around her eyes that made them appear to be sunken into her puffy face. But some of the light, the fire, had returned to her wide lavender-blue eyes.

"I don't see Gypsy. Do you see Gypsy?" Hope leaned over the porch railing. Gypsy was all Hope could talk about for weeks. Mackenzie had taken Hope to the feed store so she could buy a large tub of special treats for all the horses.

"She's in one of those trailers, kiddo… They wouldn't

leave her behind…" Mackenzie saw Dylan through the windshield of Aggie's truck and, as was usual nowadays, her pulse quickened. She was simply head over heels crazy for that man. She could finally relate to the lyrics of sappy love songs and the tortured words of poems. She just *loved* him. He was her special somebody.

Dylan hopped out of the truck. He lifted up his arms with a tired, happy smile. "We did it. We're here!"

Aggie was already barking orders, directing traffic and setting the second phase of the move into motion. She had already moved some of her items into the office and she had spent quite a bit of time on the farm, getting familiar with their new digs.

"What can we do to help?" Aunt Gerri's bright blue eyes were dancing with excitement. Dylan turned to look at the cars, and trucks, and trailers and people. The farm was *alive* again.

"Just sit back and watch the show…" Dylan kissed his aunt on the cheek. To Hope, he asked, "Ready to see Gypsy?"

Hope nodded and slipped her hand into his hand.

Mackenzie and Dylan caught each other's eyes and held. "I'm going to help Gerri with the food. I'm sure everyone's going to be starved…"

With one last smile, a loving smile meant just for Mackenzie, Dylan took his daughter to the last trailer in the line. Hope was like the rock star of the day; this was the first time many people from Pegasus had had an opportunity to see her since she'd been in the hospital. But, because Hope was fresh off chemotherapy, and her immune system was still weak, all the people who wanted to greet her and hug her had to keep their distance. Hope's recovery was still too fragile for her to be exposed to viruses right now. It was already a risk to have her around this many people, but neither Mackenzie nor he had the heart to tell her that she couldn't be a part of this day.

Hope ran up to the last trailer when she spotted Gypsy. She stood on tiptoe so she could touch the white star on the mare's forehead.

"Hi, there, Gyps…you've got a new home now. A better home, with really big pastures and lots of grass and your very own stall…"

Hope looked at him. "She looks okay, doesn't she?"

"Yeah…I think she looks great."

"Hey! Axel!" Wearing faded jeans, motorcycle boots, a plain white V-neck T-shirt and a black paisley bandanna on her head, Jordan appeared from behind one of the moving trucks.

"Jordan…I didn't know you were going to make it today," Dylan said.

"Are you kidding me? Do you think I'd miss a chance to hang with my favorite second cousin?" Jordan reached out, gave Hope's hand a quick squeeze before she moved back a couple of steps to keep a safe distance.

Hope smiled up at Jordan. "I like your bandanna."

"I like yours." Jordan returned the compliment and then looked around. "Man…this is quite a posse you've assembled."

"I know…I still can't believe it," he agreed. "Mackenzie's in the house with my aunt if you want to say hi."

"Yeah…let me do that before you put me to work." Jordan blew Hope a kiss before she headed toward the house.

Jordan followed the sound of voices and the smell of good food cooking back to the kitchen. Mackenzie and Gerri were laughing and talking when she showed up. Mackenzie greeted her with a warm hug and then she introduced her to Dylan's aunt.

"Did Ian come, too?"

Jordan propped her hip against the counter, crossed her arms casually in front of her. "No. He hates crowds."

"That's too bad." Mackenzie frowned.

"Ian has always been a bit of an introvert," Gerri said. "He actually got a little worse when all the girls started to chase him senior year..."

"Hey...that's right!" Jordan exclaimed. "You know Ian!"

"Like he was another one of my own..." Gerri nodded. "He didn't really start to come out of his shell until he went to college. Modeling helped. But, now, with his eyes, I'm afraid he's slipping back into his old ways..."

Jordan leaned down, elbow on the counter, chin propped up by her hand. "I'm actually thinking about getting him a service dog. He'd die before he used a cane..."

"A service dog's a good idea. Get him a man's dog, like a black Lab. That would suit him." Gerri slid a pan of cookies into the oven.

"I'm gonna do it." Jordan nodded. Then she changed the subject. "So...I hear you're *engaged* now?"

Lately, Mackenzie had been blushing. And, now she was at it again. Mackenzie smiled shyly. "Dylan asked me to marry him."

"My nephew knows a good thing when he sees it..." Gerri smiled warmly at Mackenzie.

"I'm really happy for you... He's a really great guy." Jordan straightened upright. "Is Hope over the moon?"

"Totally over the moon..." Mackenzie put a bowl in the sink and ran water into it. "We already got our marriage license."

Jordan's jaw dropped. "Uh...*wow*! Where's the fire?"

"Dylan doesn't want to wait," she said. "And I guess I don't want to wait either. Dylan wants to get married here, in front of the old oak tree behind the house."

"Well, more power to you. I'd love to do a quickie wedding, but Mom is pulling out all the stops back home. Luckily, all I have to do is sit back, let her do her thing and approve the stuff she emails me."

"Aunt Barb knows how to throw a party…"

"She does…but honestly, Ian'd love to just elope, but he promised me we'd get married in Montana and I'm gonna hold him to it…" Jordan popped a chocolate chip into her mouth. "You've got to let me and Jo take you shopping for a dress. Jo dies for that kind of stuff. She's still trying to manifest a proposal out of *Brice*. Yuck." Jordan shuddered. "You *are* going to invite the Brand clan to this shindig, right? If you don't, trust me, you'll be able to hear Mom's hissy fit all the way from Montana!"

After the horses were all settled, the feed was in the new feed room and the tack was put away in the new tack room, his aunt's house filled up with hungry folks who had been working all day. One of the front rooms was set up with long tables for an all-you-can-eat buffet. Some of the food was brought in, but most of the food was home-cooked by Gerri. With their paper plates and plastic cups in tow, it was standing room only in Gerri's organ room. For this special occasion, and particularly for Hope, Gerri turned on the Christmas-tree lights.

"I haven't seen her this happy in years," Dylan whispered to Mackenzie. Mackenzie was perched on the arm of a chair and he was standing next to her. Hope had taken the seat of honor next to his aunt on the organ bench.

"Now…" Aunt Gerri said to her audience while she looked through a songbook. "I like to start off playing 'Do Re Mi' to limber up my fingers. I usually play it two times 'cause it has all the notes in the scale, plus you've got sharps and flats and it's a gay little tune so it puts me in a real good cheerful mood." Hope looked happy; she had even agreed to wear the white, protective mask that she hated just so she wouldn't miss out on the fun.

"And—" Aunt Gerri smiled at Hope "—once I'm all warmed up, I'll play 'Count Your Blessings' just for you!"

"Come outside with me for a minute." Dylan reached for her hand.

Mackenzie linked her fingers with his as he led her to the kitchen and through the back door. They walked down the back steps, across the yard, to the beautiful three-hundred-year-old oak tree that was growing behind Gerri's house. Under the tree, Dylan kissed her, slow and sweet.

"I love it here." Mackenzie was wrapped up securely in Dylan's arms, his chin resting lightly on the top of her head.

"Me, too…"

"I can't wait to marry you under this tree…." She rested her head on his shoulder, listened to his strong, steady heartbeat.

"Have I told you lately how much I love you?"

Mackenzie smiled. "Yes. You have. And I love you."

Dylan loosened his arms, took a small step back. Mackenzie looked so pretty in this soft, golden early-evening light.

"There's something I need to do…" Dylan knelt down at her feet, took her hand in his hand.

"What are you doing?" Mackenzie laughed nervously. "You already *asked* me to marry you!"

"You deserve a better proposal than that, Mackenzie." Dylan stared up into her eyes. "You're so beautiful to me, do you know that? I look at you and you take my breath away. I can't remember what my life was like before I met you…before I met Hope…and I don't want to remember, because none of that stuff matters anymore. You're everything to me, Mackenzie. Will you marry me?"

Dylan pulled a ring out of his front pocket and poised it at the tip of her ring finger.

"You know I will…" There was an emotional catch in Mackenzie's words.

Dylan slipped the heart-shaped diamond engagement ring onto her finger.

"It's a heart, Dylan!" Mackenzie admired the ring. "I collect hearts!"

"I remember." Dylan had her in his arms once again. He kissed her and she kissed him. They embraced in the spot where they would one day say their vows. They embraced in the soft dusky light with the sound of nickering horses drifting up from the barns. It was a perfect, stolen moment between two people who had fallen in love.

Night had fallen on the farm and there were only a few vehicles parked in the grassy area next to his aunt's house. The food had been packed up, the dishes cleaned, the tables broken down to be put back in storage and the trash had been removed. His aunt was taking requests on the organ for some of the folks who were too tired to get up and drive home. Dylan was sandwiched between Mackenzie and Hope on the porch swing. Hope was tuckered out from her day; she was leaning against him, eyes closed as they gently swung back and forth on the swing.

"I want to shave my head." Hope spoke after a long stretch of silence.

"What?" Mackenzie leaned forward to look at her daughter. "Why?"

"Because it's falling out anyway…" Hope said. "And, I'm tired of it falling in my food when I'm trying to eat."

"Are you sure?" Mackenzie asked.

Hope nodded. "Yeah…it's time."

Dylan hugged his daughter closer. "I feel like shaving my head, too. You can shave mine at the same time."

Hope perked up. "*Really*? I can?"

"No..." Mackenzie objected.

"Sure...why not?" Dylan ran his hand over his hair. "I need a haircut. That way we can both grow our hair out for the wedding."


Hope had been spending time with Dylan at his beach house. She loved the beach and she loved spending time with him. This switch was hard on Ray and Charlie because they were used to watching Hope, but their lives were changing. In fact—Mackenzie hadn't really discussed it with Ray yet—Dylan wanted them to live in his house after the wedding. She loved Balboa Park and didn't want to leave, but Hope was so happy at the beach. It was hard for her to say no.

"Where is everyone?" Mackenzie took the key out of the door. "Hello?"

She dropped her tote on the kitchen counter. There were two dirty plates on the island, not in the sink. There was a glass on the counter without a coaster. Mackenzie put the dishes and glass in the sink.

"Hello?" She checked in the den next. Maybe Dylan and Hope had gone down to the beach. But when she checked the French doors leading out to the deck, they were still locked. When she didn't find them on the lower floor, she headed up the stairs.

"Dylan! Hope!"

"We're up here!" Dylan shouted from his bathroom on the third floor.

Mackenzie heard her daughter laughing loudly. The higher she climbed, the louder a suspicious buzzing sound became.

"What are the two of you doing in here?" Mackenzie stood in the doorway, horrified.

Dylan was sitting cross-legged on the floor; Hope had a large electric clipper in her hand. Dylan's button-down shirt, his pants and his fancy marble floor were covered with his hair. Hope had used the clippers to buzz a thick, crooked line from his forehead to the back of his neck.

"I'm the barber and this is my client," Hope explained.

"Have you looked at yourself in the mirror?" Mackenzie asked him.

"I'm waiting to be surprised." Dylan winked at her.

"I have no doubt it will be a surprise," she said.

Dylan was blissfully unaware of how horrible his usually perfect hair looked. "Come join us… We've missed you."

"I've missed you…" Mackenzie leaned back against the doorjamb. "You do realize that you've come over to the dark side, right? Do you know how long it's going to take to get all of those little hairs up off the floor?"

"That's why he has a maid," Hope told her as if she said the word *maid* every day and twice on Sundays.

Mackenzie took a step inside the bathroom, arms crossed over her chest. She frowned severely at her fiancé and Hope. "Um…that would be a *no.* Dylan, we're not going to teach her that. When the two of you are done, the two of you are going to clean this up."

"Okay, Mom…"

"Okay, sweetheart…"

Hope proudly buzzed off the right side of Dylan's hair. Mackenzie covered her eyes. "I can't watch this."

Mackenzie left them to their little shaving party, grabbed a glass of wine and went out onto the deck. Her mind drifted back to their first date. She hadn't even considered Dylan date material at that point and now she was engaged to the man. Life had a way of surprising you all the time.

"It feels really cold up there now." Dylan walked out onto the deck, rubbing his shorn hair. "What do you think? Do you still want to marry me?"

Mackenzie stood up and then reached up so she could rub her hand across his shaved head. "It's like peach fuzz now..."

"Peach fuzz? And here I was thinking that I looked like a tough guy."

Mackenzie shook her head and smiled. She hugged him. The fact that he had let Hope shave his head to make their daughter feel more comfortable about shaving her own head touched her. She liked him better with his hair, but she loved him more with his head shaved.

Hope came out on the deck and the three of them went down to the beach for a walk. Mackenzie knew full well that neither of them had bothered to clean up the hair in the bathroom, but she didn't say so. The truth was, she didn't want to miss a moment with them tonight. They could always clean tomorrow.

## Chapter Sixteen

Several months had passed since the Pegasus gang had moved to Aunt Gerri's farm. Hope was still in remission and her hair had grown back enough to be styled into a cute pixie cut like her cousin Jordan's. Mackenzie was busier than ever between the bakery and the wedding plans. Dylan was an involved groom, which made the planning more fun than a chore. The invitations had been sent and many of her Montana relatives had RSVP'd. Her dad and Jett were coming down from Paradise with her nieces. Hope, Jordan, Josephine, Rayna and Charlie had helped her pick out a beautiful lace fit-and-flare wedding dress with a sweetheart neckline, capped sleeves and crystal embellishments. She had worried that she wouldn't be able to find a gown that would work with her curves, but she had. This dress gave her a perfect hour-glass figure while smoothing out the bulges and bumps. In all of the weeks leading up to the wedding, Mackenzie had been stressed out about the details, but she was never nervous about marrying Dylan. And now that the big day had actually arrived, she was excited to see her family and for Dylan to see her in her dress, but she still wasn't nervous.

The two of them had spent the night at Aunt Gerri's house, while Hope stayed with Rayna and Charlie. Dylan, having an old-fashioned moment, insisted that they sleep in separate rooms so he wouldn't see her before the ceremony. The morning of the wedding, Mackenzie awakened missing him. They had agreed not to move in together until after the wedding, and with their work and Hope, it wasn't always easy to find time to be alone. Mackenzie slipped on her bathrobe and tiptoed down the hallway to Dylan's room. She quietly opened the door and sneaked in. Dylan, as usual, was on top of the sheets, flat on his back. He was bare-chested but had worn pajama bottoms to bed. He was snoring lightly; she wanted her visit to be a surprise and now it would be.

Smiling at her own stealth, Mackenzie sneaked over to the bed.

"Dylan…" she whispered.

Dylan grumbled, stretched and rolled over onto his side. She poked his shoulder.

"Dylan…" This time a little bit more loudly.

Caught off guard and groggy, Dylan opened his eyes. When he realized she was standing by the bed, he smiled at her.

"Hey, baby…" he said sleepily. "What're you doing?"

"Happy wedding day…" She smiled at him.

Dylan yawned loudly while he roughed up his short hair, grown back now from his buzz cut, trying to wake up. He rubbed the sleep out of his eyes, and when the fog started to lift, he realized that this was the morning of the day he was going to marry Mackenzie.

"Hey…" Dylan propped himself up on his elbow. "What are you doing in my room? It's bad luck for me to see you."

Mackenzie shook her head. "No…it's bad luck for you to see me in my wedding dress before the ceremony. I'm not *in* my wedding dress…"

There was a saucy glint in her eyes as she slowly untied the belt on her robe. She opened the robe and let it fall to the floor. The robe was the only thing she had put on to come to Dylan's room. And now she was standing before him, completely naked.

Dylan's eyes drank her in. She was such a sexy, beautiful woman. He loved her curvaceous Marilyn Monroe figure: the large natural breasts, the small waist, the flare of her voluptuous hips. He loved her inside and out and he wanted her all the time.

"How do you feel about your luck now?" she asked him seductively.

Dylan didn't hide the fact that he was admiring every inch of her naked body. "I think I'm the luckiest man alive."

Mackenzie laughed softly; he held out his hand to her. Her hand in his, and still standing, Dylan leaned over and pressed a kiss on her rounded belly.

"Your body's changing already." He rested his free hand on her stomach, over their growing child.

She smiled, nodded and placed her hand over his. "A little. We won't be able to keep the secret much longer."

"We'll tell everyone after the honeymoon." He swung his legs over the side of the bed, pulled her between his thighs and hugged her close.

His head nestled between her breasts and Mackenzie kissed the top of his head lovingly. They had discovered that she was pregnant soon after Hope was released from the hospital. Once she was past the first trimester, she would feel safe to share the news. But, for now, it was a sweet, private secret that she could share with her husband-to-be.

"How are you feeling?" Dylan knew that Mackenzie had started to have minor bouts with morning sickness.

"I feel great today." She pulled back a little. "I'm marrying you."

His hands began to explore her back, her hips, and the moment took a turn to the sensual. Dylan's mouth was on her breast, sending wonderful tingling to the most sensitive part of her body. She tilted her head back, raked her fingers through his hair and savored his attention unabashedly. This was her man, and there was everything right about their lovemaking.

"Do you want to go for a ride?" Dylan asked her suggestively.

Mackenzie laughed as she always did at his not-so-subtle sexual innuendos. She stripped off his underwear, knelt between his thighs and took him into her mouth. Dylan closed his eyes; he braced himself back on his arms and groaned, long and low. Dylan reached for her, hunger in his eyes.

"Come here…" Dylan lay on his back with a smile; hands behind his head and shaft hard and erect and ready for her pleasure.

Without any pretense, Mackenzie sunk down and took him as deep within her body as she could.

"Oh…" The inside of her body was tight, and wet, and so incredibly warm.

And, then she began to move. Dylan watched her ride him; she was a thing of beauty. Her head was tilted back, her lips parted as she moaned with pleasure. Her breasts, so round and full, with pink nipples moved sensually as she rotated her hips. He could feel her hair, long and loose, brushing his thighs. Dylan felt her start to tense, and he knew instinctively that she was starting to peak. He grabbed onto her hips, thrusting inside her faster and harder.

Mackenzie collapsed forward and tried to stifle the sound of her orgasm in his neck. Her orgasm triggered his and they held on to each other tightly as the waves of ecstasy crashed over their bodies. Dylan rolled her over onto her back and smiled down at her.

"God, I love you…"

She reached up to touch his face. "I love you, too, Dylan. More than I can say."

She had laid in his arms until she heard cars, *plural*, heading up the driveway. She had peeked out the blinds to discover a caravan of cars heading their way. It looked like the Montana Brands had arrived, along with the makeup artist, and *she* was still naked, post coitus, in her fiancé's bed! She quickly put her robe back on, and after a lengthy goodbye kiss, she sneaked back to her own bedroom.

"Hey, Mackenzie!" Jordan banged on her door. "We're here. Open up!"

Mackenzie had taken a shower to rinse off the evidence of their lovemaking and now she was back in her robe. She opened the door and Jordan reached out, grabbed her wrist and dragged her down the stairs.

"Come *on*!" Jordan wouldn't let go of her hand. "Dylan's aunt wants us to use the sitting room downstairs to get ready. We can close it off completely and that way the groom can't sneak a peek before you say *I do*!"

Laughing now, Mackenzie was whisked into the sitting room and the doors were closed behind her. Thanks to Ian's connections, a celebrity hairstylist and makeup artist would be on the scene later to do her hair. Her cousin

Josephine Brand was unzipping the garment bag holding her violet bridesmaid dress. Stylish, classic Josephine had helped her with every detail of the wedding, from dresses to tent rentals and everything in between.

Josephine stopped what she was doing and ran over to give her a hug. "Mackenzie! Have you seen the ceremony setup? It's gorgeous!"

Josephine was Jordan's twin, but when they stood side by side, it wasn't easy to know that. Jordan wore her hair short and switched colors every other month, while Josephine wore her hair long and wavy and naturally golden-brown.

Now that her relatives had arrived, the quiet of the farmhouse was shattered. In the hallway, Mackenzie could hear Aunt Gerri greeting her family in from Montana. She heard footsteps coming down the creaky wooden stairs, and then heard Dylan introducing himself to her family. The front door opened and the male voices disappeared. With flare, Barbara Brand slid the doors open wide and joined them in the sitting room.

"Oh, Mackenzie!" Her aunt Barb's arms were extended toward her for a hug. "I'm so happy that we're here to see you get married!"

She had always had a special connection with Jordan and Josephine's mom. Aunt Barb never forgot her on special holidays, sending her special little gifts. Many of the hearts in her heart collection had been sent to her by Aunt Barb.

Mackenzie hugged her aunt so tightly. She was the closest thing to a mom she had today, and she was so happy that they had made the trip all the way from their ranch in Montana to attend.

Barbara, very chic and trim, her platinum hair slicked back into her trademark chignon, smiled lovingly at her niece. She pulled a small box out of her Hermès bag. "Your uncle and I want you to have this… Your grandmother wore this on her wedding day…"

Mackenzie opened the aged, blue velvet box. Inside was a perfect string of antique pearls. She had seen these very pearls in a picture of her grandmother on her wedding day.

"Oh, Aunt Barb…they're beautiful. Thank you."

Her aunt helped her put on the pearls. "You're beautiful. They suit you."

Her cousins gathered around to admire the necklace, complimenting her and assuring her that it was going to go beautifully with her gown. Aunt Gerri came in with a plate of food, and then they started to prepare her for the wedding in earnest. She watched from her chair as trucks pulled up with chairs, tables and food. Her makeup was professionally applied; her hair was swept up away from her face with long, loose curls down her back. Dylan was going to love her hair this way.

She had never been fussed over so much before, but it wasn't half-bad. It was actually kind of fun and the end result would make Dylan a very happy man. Rayna, who was going to perform the ceremony, arrived with Charlie and Hope. Hope bounced into the room excitedly and hugged her mom right away.

"Look what Dad gave me!" Hope held out her hand and showed Mackenzie a ring with a small heart-shaped amethyst in the center.

"It's beautiful, just like you…" Mackenzie hugged her daughter hard. "Jordan's going to help you get ready, okay?"

There was so much commotion in the room, especially after Rayna and Charlie arrived, that no one noticed that she hadn't touched her champagne. They laughed and they talked and they reminisced and they all got gussied up in their beautiful dresses. Hope's flower-girl dress was lace with a satin sash and lavender flower embellishments; she was beaming because she was allowed to have a hint of makeup applied. When they were all dressed, Josephine, Jordan and Charlie looked gorgeous in tea-length lavender chiffon dresses, strapless with sweetheart necklines. The women in her life gathered around her and helped her put on her wedding dress.

She worried that her tiny baby bump would make the dress too tight around the waist, but it was a perfect fit.

"Oh, my goodness, you're so special…" Aunt Gerri admired her. "You're the best thing that happened to Dylan, Mackenzie, and I love you. I hope the two of you will have fifty years together like Bill and I did…"

The ceremony was set to start in less than thirty minutes. Mackenzie was filled with nervous excitement and she couldn't wait to see Dylan. She stood in front of the full-length mirror that had been brought especially for her, and she couldn't believe that the attractive woman in the reflection was actually *her*. Her dress, her hair, her makeup…the pearl necklace…made such a pretty picture. She was a bride. She was Dylan's bride.

Barbara slid open the pocket doors leading out to the foyer. Hank Brand, her uncle and her mother's older brother, was talking with Aunt Gerri in the foyer.

Uncle Hank was lanky and tall; he had thick silver hair and deep-set blue eyes. He owned and operated Bent Tree Cattle Ranch in Montana and had done for as long as she could remember. He was wearing a navy blue suit, and his cowboy hat was in his hand, cowboy boots on his feet.

"You look just like Hope did when you were her age…" Hank studied her face seriously. He was a hard man, a tough man, but there was always a kindness beneath his weathered exterior. Hank had been very close with her mother, and she could tell that it still stung, all these years later, that his baby sister had died.

As the time for the ceremony to start approached, and the majority of the guests had arrived and been seated by the old oak tree, Mackenzie went back into the drawing room so Dylan wouldn't see her before the ceremony. Alone in the room, Mackenzie put her hand on her stomach and closed her eyes. She needed to harness her roiling emotions; she could feel tears of joy and anticipation and relief gathering behind her eyes.

"You are not going to ruin your makeup!" Mackenzie whispered to herself sternly.

The door to the sitting room slid open and her father poked his head in. "I've been playing heck to find you! This place is like a maze."

"Dad!" Relieved to see him, Mackenzie threw herself into her father's big, burly arms. "Oh, my goodness! You *shaved*?"

Jim Bronson was a hefty, barrel-chested man who had worn a thick unruly beard since he had retired from the auto industry. She hadn't seen the lower half of her father's face for over a decade.

Jim smiled self-consciously as he touched his fleshy, freshly shaven face. "I have more chins now than I'd like to know about, but I wanted to look nice for your pictures."

"Thank you, Dad…"

"Now, I know I'm a handsome devil like this…" Jim said with a spark of humor in his deeply set brown eyes. "But don't go getting all attached. I start growing my beard back tonight."

Mackenzie laughed; she touched a couple of nicks on his chin. The lower half of his face was whiter than the part of his face that had always been exposed to the sunlight. "That's okay…I don't think you're all that good at shaving."

Jim captured her hand, kissed it, then stepped back and twirled her under his arm just the way he had when she was a little girl.

"You look like your mom on our wedding day." Jim's expression was more serious now, his eyes watery. Mackenzie hadn't seen her father this close to tears since her mother's funeral.

Mackenzie hugged her father again, careful not to get makeup on his white tuxedo shirt. Jim accepted the hug and then, as he always did, changed the mood from serious to joking. He stepped back and twisted from side to side.

"I'm hurt that you didn't even bother to mention my getup." Jim raised his arms to show off his black tuxedo. "Do you think it's easy to find a monkey suit in extra-big and not-so-tall?"

The door slid open and Josephine poked her head into the room. "Dylan's about to take his place and then you'll come out."

Jim looked down at his daughter proudly. He offered his arm to her and asked, "Ready?"

Mackenzie accepted her father's arm. "Absolutely."

Dylan looked out of his boyhood bedroom window at all the people taking their seats. He would be a married man soon, and he'd been looking forward to this day for months.

"Can you believe I'm taking the plunge before you?" Dylan asked Ian, his best friend and best man.

Ian was sitting in a chair next to the bed. "I didn't see this one coming…"

Dylan smiled. "Do you have the rings?"

"Right here in my pocket."

Mackenzie had wanted a small intimate ceremony and

she had wanted simple, classic gold bands. He would have preferred rings that were a little more ornate, but in the end, he just wanted her to be happy.

Dylan saw Rayna take her position beneath the oak tree, and heard his aunt start to play the organ. As they had rehearsed, that was his signal to come down for the ceremony.

"They're ready for us…"

"Showtime…" Dylan stood up, shrugged on his jacket and headed down the stairs.

Once outside, Dylan walked down the aisle and took his position next to Rayna, who smiled warmly at him. He was glad that he had Ian to stand with him. Most of the guests were Mackenzie's family from Montana. He, on the other hand, didn't have much family. He had half brothers and half sisters from his father's side that he'd never met. All he really had was Aunt Gerri and Ian. But, after today, he had a whole new family; and most important, he would have Mackenzie and Hope. The organ had been moved outside for the ceremony, and when his aunt began to play the classic wedding march, he knew his moment to finally marry Mackenzie had arrived. A hush fell over the guests, and Dylan actually felt his knees buckle.

First, he saw his beautiful Hope walking down the aisle toward him throwing petals. Over the last months, she had bounced back from her bout in the hospital. Her pixie-cut hairstyle fit her round, freckled face perfectly. And she looked so pretty in her lace dress and lavender sash. Down the aisle came Charlie, the matron of honor, and then Jordan and her twin sister, Josephine. And then finally, finally, he saw Mackenzie and her dad poised to come down the aisle toward him. He was awestruck by the beauty of his bride. He always thought she was pretty, but today, in that dress, she was an angel in white lace. The crystals on her veil sparkled in the late-morning sunlight as she walked slowly toward him carrying a bouquet of purple orchids. Through the delicate fabric of the veil, Dylan met her eyes. And, for a split second, they were the only two people in the world.

"Who gives this woman to this man?"

"I do," Jim Bronson bellowed. Mackenzie pressed her lips together for a moment so she wouldn't laugh out loud at the sound her father's booming voice disrupting the otherwise serene, tranquil setting.

Jim lifted the veil off his daughter's face and kissed her lightly on the cheek. To Dylan he said roughly, "Take good care of her."

"I will, sir. I love her." Dylan shook her father's hand and then reached out for hers.

"You are beautiful…" Dylan said to his bride.

Mackenzie's eyes were full of love for him. "I love you…"

Beneath that sprawling oak tree, and before a small group of their close family and friends, Dylan and Mackenzie exchanged their vows. The ceremony was simple and quiet and traditional, as were their vows to each other.

Rayna performed her duties admirably, but there were a couple of moments when she needed to calm her own emotions; she was so happy that her dear friend had finally met her match. Mackenzie handed her bouquet to Hope, and Ian handed the rings to Dylan. With their wedding bands securely in place, hands clasped together, Rayna said the words they had been waiting to hear.

"By the power vested in me, I now pronounce you man and wife. Dylan, you may kiss your beautiful bride…"

They leaned in to each other.

"I told them no lipstick so you can kiss me for real," his wife whispered to him.

And he did kiss her for real. He took her in his arms and kissed her on the lips, and then he hugged her so tightly that he let her know that he never wanted to let her go.

"Ladies and gentlemen, Dylan and Mackenzie Axel!"

Mackenzie took Hope's hand and the three of them walked up the aisle, as a family, while the crowd cheered for them. It had been a perfect ceremony, on a perfect California day, and Mackenzie believed to her core that this was the start of a long and successful marriage. They held the reception in a large tent beside the house. There was dancing and eating and drinking and pictures being taken. Mackenzie couldn't remember a day when she had laughed so much.

"Are you having a good time?" Dylan had just danced with Hope and now he was back in her arms.

"This is the best day of my life…" She laughed as he dipped her over his arm.

"It's almost time for us to leave for the honeymoon, you know…"

"I know." Mackenzie frowned at him playfully. "Why won't you tell me where we're going?"

"It's a surprise." Dylan twirled her around to make her laugh again. "But I'll give you a hint…it's warm, it's an island and we are taking the private company jet."

"Sounds like heaven…" Mackenzie said. "But anywhere is heaven when I'm with you."

Finally, Dylan had to pull her away from her friends and family. They did have a flight to catch. Mackenzie was having such a blast that she hated to leave, but she knew it was time. Her last duty as the bride was to throw the bouquet. All of the single women bunched together and Mackenzie counted, "one, two, three…" and tossed the bouquet over her shoulder.

Without trying very hard to catch it, the bouquet landed in Josephine's hands. Surprised, she looked over at her longtime boyfriend, Brice, whose expression didn't change when he saw her catch the bouquet.

"Josephine…you're next!" Mackenzie said.

"We'll see…" Josephine lifted the flowers up for Brice to see before she brought them to her nose to catch the sweet scent of the purple orchids.

After Josephine caught the bouquet, Mackenzie and Dylan hugged and kissed Hope goodbye with a promise to bring her something back from their honeymoon. They climbed into the backseat of Ian's chauffeured Bentley, rolled down the window and waved to their friends and family who had gathered in the driveway. Aunt Gerri came up to the car and kissed both of them.

"I love you both…" Her eyes were damp with unshed tears.

"Thank you, Aunt Gerri…for today…for everything," Dylan said.

To Dylan she said, "Bill always kissed me good-night and told me that he loved me. You do that for Mackenzie and you'll have fifty years like we did."

Gerri had the last word before the window was rolled up and the car drove away. Mackenzie waved through the tinted back window of the car until the house was out of sight. Dylan draped his arm around her shoulders and pulled her into his body.

"Are you happy?" he asked her.

"So happy…" She leaned her head back on his shoulder.

She was Dylan's wife now; he was her husband. They had a daughter and another child on the way. Mackenzie turned in his arms so she could kiss her husband. Dylan kissed her sweetly, gently, his hand on her face.

"Have I told you lately that I love you?" His eyes locked with hers.

"Yes…" she said. "But tell me again."

\* \* \* \* \*

# COMING NEXT MONTH FROM

**H HARLEQUIN®**

# SPECIAL EDITION

## Available February 17, 2015

### #2389 MENDOZA'S SECRET FORTUNE
*The Fortunes of Texas: Cowboy Country* • by Marie Ferrarella
Rachel Robinson never counted herself among the beauties of Horseback Hollow, Texas...until handsome brothers Matteo and Cisco Mendoza began competing for her attention! But it's Matteo who catches her eye and proves to be the most ardent suitor. He might just convince Rachel to leave her past behind her and start life anew—with him!

### #2390 A CONARD COUNTY BABY
*Conard County: The Next Generation* • by Rachel Lee
Pregnant Hope Conroy is fleeing a dark past when she lands in Conard County, Wyoming, where Jim "Cash" Cashford, a single dad with a feisty teenager on his hands, resides. When Cash stumbles across Hope, he's desperate for help, so he hires the Texan beauty to help rein in his daughter. As the bond between Cash and Hope flourishes, there might just be another Conard County family in the making...

### #2391 A SECOND CHANCE AT CRIMSON RANCH • by Michelle Major
Olivia Wilder isn't eager for love after her husband ran off with his secretary, leaving her lost and lonely. So when she scores a dance with handsome Logan Travers at his brother's wedding, her thoughts aren't on romance or falling for the rancher. A former Colorado wild boy, Logan is drawn to Olivia, but fears he's not good enough for her. Can two individuals who have been burned by love in the past find their own happily-ever-after on the range?

### #2392 THE BACHELOR'S BABY DILEMMA
*Family Renewal* • by Sheri WhiteFeather
The last thing Tanner Quinn wants is a baby. Ever since his infant sister died, the handsome horseman has avoided little ones like the plague—but now he's the guardian of his newborn niece! What's a man to do? Tanner calls in his ex-girlfriend Candy McCall to help. The nurturing nanny is wonderful with the baby—and with Tanner, too. Although this avowed bachelor has sworn off marriage, Candy might just be sweet enough to convince him otherwise.

### #2393 FROM CITY GIRL TO RANCHER'S WIFE • by Ami Weaver
When chef Josie Callahan loses everything to her devious ex-fiancé, she leaves town, hightailing it to Montana. There, Josie takes refuge in a temporary job...on the ranch of a sexy former country star. Luke Ryder doesn't need a beautiful woman tantalizing him—especially one who won't last a New York minute on a ranch. He's also a private man who doesn't want a stranger poking around...even if she gets him to open his heart to love!

### #2394 HER PERFECT PROPOSAL • by Lynne Marshall
Journalist Lilly Matsuda is eager to get her hands dirty as a reporter in Heartlandia, Oregon. The locals aren't crazy about her, though—Lilly even gets pulled over by hunky cop Gunnar Norling! But the two bond. As Gunnar quickly becomes more than just a source to Lilly, conflicts of interest soon arise. Can the policeman and his lady love find their own happy ending in Heartlandia?

**YOU CAN FIND MORE INFORMATION ON UPCOMING HARLEQUIN® TITLES, FREE EXCERPTS AND MORE AT WWW.HARLEQUIN.COM.**

HSECNM0215

SPECIAL EXCERPT FROM

**H** HARLEQUIN®

## SPECIAL EDITION

*Matteo Mendoza is used to playing second fiddle
to his brother Cisco…but not this time. Beautiful
Rachel Robinson intrigues both siblings, but Matteo
is determined to win her heart. Rachel can't resist the
handsome pilot, but she's afraid her family secrets might
haunt her chances at love. Can this Texan twosome find
their very own happily-ever-after on the range?*

*Read on for a sneak preview of
**MENDOZA'S SECRET FORTUNE** by USA TODAY
bestselling author Marie Ferrarella, the third book in
**THE FORTUNES OF TEXAS: COWBOY COUNTRY**
continuity!*

\*\*\*

Matteo knew he should be leaving—and had most likely
already overstayed—but he found himself wanting to linger
just a few more seconds in her company.

"I just wanted to tell you one more time that I had a very
nice time tonight," he told Rachel.

She surprised him—and herself when she came right down
to it—by saying, "Show me."

Matteo looked at her, confusion in his eyes. Had he heard
wrong? And what did she mean by that, anyway?

"What?"

"Show me," Rachel repeated.

"How?" he asked, not exactly sure he understood what she
was getting at.